Praise for *Blues*

"What to do with Tom Jerome, that classic American on the make, edging past his prime with two basic urges intact: *here* and *now*? I laughed hard and even blushed a bit, but most of all I admired the cunning and wisdom of this enchanting new hero and his creator!"

– Lee W. Doty, author of *Tidal Kin and Last Casualty*

"With the grace of Keats—whose poetic presence gives this volume its focus and its lively force—Altman whips lusty and literate sonnets into a sweeping, scary, and sensational masterpiece. Great, surprising fun!"

**– William Lanouette,
author of *Genius in the Shadows: A Biography of Leo Szilard,
the Man Behind the Bomb* and *The Triumph of the Amateurs:
The Rise, Ruin, and Banishment of Professional
Rowing in the Gilded Age***

"As in any good film noir, our hero gets clunked on the head by love. The catch? His muse is fed up with playing the femme fatale for a bunch of Roman gangsters. Like all the players in *Blues for the Muse,* she wants something more. That's just what she gets, and so will you in this spritely, droll, and engrossing tale of romance gone hilariously wrong."

– Sollace Mitchell, director of *Call Me and Row Your Boat*

"Sonnets have packed a wallop in recent literature, a movement Stephen Altman's dazzling sonnet sequence furthers with film-noir vengeance. More than just a sexy tale of gangsters and femme fatales, Altman's sonnets are serial love poems in the convicted spirit of *Berryman's Sonnets* by John Berryman and the recent *frank:sonnets* by Dianne Seuss."

**– Ed Zahniser, Poet Laureate of Shepherdstown,
West Virginia and author of *Mall-hopping with the
Great I AM* and *Confidence in Being***

Blues for the Muse

STEPHEN ALTMAN

SILVER TREE PRESS
SHEPHERDSTOWN, WEST VIRGINIA

Blues for the Muse

Text and Illustrations Copyright © 2021 Stephen Altman

All Rights Reserved

For information about this title or to order other books and/or electronic media, contact the publisher:

SILVER TREE PRESS
SHEPHERDSTOWN, WEST VIRGINIA

silvertreepress.wv@gmail.com

ISBN: 978-1-7374447-0-1 (Hardcover)
ISBN: 978-1-7374447-1-8 (Trade Paperback)
ISBN: 978-1-7374447-2-5 (eBook)

Cover illustration © Jean Gauthier.
Assistance with interior illustrations courtesy of Tom and Jared at Studio 105.

Blues for the Muse is a work of fiction. All of the characters, organizations, and events portrayed in this novel are either products of the author's imagination or are used fictitiously. Where real-life figures appear, the situations, incidents, and dialogues concerning those persons are entirely fictional and are not intended to change the completely fictional nature of the work.

Printed in the United States of America

A te

This, in Keats's present mood, seemed a desirable challenge—to write in the style of the old poets and on old themes, with the taste and spirit of a modern writer, but without the personal and ephemeral themes that seemed to engage modern poets.

— **Robert Gittings** on the
poet in early 1818, in *John Keats*

PART I

PART I

1

The cemetery in Testaccio!
No sweeter place to lie when you are dead,
Though not to merely lie and rot; instead,
To live eternally where pomegranates grow,
And flowers in profusion—sun aglow
On lemon trees, cypress spires overhead.
Here Beauty's Truth, as the poet said,
And all the marble nymphs carved long ago
Are watching still, like figures on an urn,
The graves arrayed like truffles in a box.
They sing the spirit in your bones' debris.
Attend, and you who fear your end will learn
That it's impossible to mourn the clock's
Advance: It's chiming immortality.

2

Immortality! Gracious! thought Tom Jerome,
That's kinda highfalutin' for a kid from Queens.
He wore a leather jacket and designer jeans,
And Ray-Bans for that famous Roman sun. His home
These days was Hollywood; he wore
Those Ray-Bans on the Sunset Strip at night,
A tad too old, it could be argued, for
Some comely starlet. Still, Jerome just might
Run into one who liked the whole gestalt:
The movie patter, poetry, the old-guy charm.
And if it worked for him, well, who could fault
Him his success? It surely did no harm
To her or him—or any girl and boy—
To share an evening's fantasy, some scrap of joy.

3

Of course, that's "Joy, whose hand is ever at his lips
Bidding adieu": a scrap of sorrow from John Keats,
Who walked a winter on the Roman streets
Before the life fell from his fingertips.
Not only Joy, but Youth, Love, Life: each slips
Away. (The roll of my ex-wives completes
The list, Jerome would say.) A notion beats
The dark despair: If time, that chiseler, chips
Away our joys—indeed, leaves none intact—
Still, time makes precious, time gives savor, so
We revel in the rising ocean wave
Because it's breaking, not despite the fact.
For this consoling thought, thought Tom Jerome, *I owe*
The kid, and went to tell him at his grave.

4

A helpful sign inside the gate advised:
Go left for Keats. But now, though near his golden boy,
Jerome turned right. His toiling heart apprised
Him of the burden of his strenuous joy.
He took his time, and climbed the terraced slope,
And found himself a bench on which he sat
And brooded sweetly on, but did not mope
About, his death. You wouldn't have expected that:
He had a cemetery temperament,
The melancholy muse inside his head
That made of every moment some huge event
In this, *The Life of Tom Jerome.* He had no dread
Of anything but ordinariness.
And then he saw the woman in the azure dress.

5

A man was being laid to rest, and he
Had friends, and all were clad in mourning hue,
But at the margin of the mourners she
Appeared, arrayed in iridescent blue.
It was as if an ibis—something rare
And unexpected—had alighted in
Their midst. The regal neck, the lifted chin,
The elegant indifference. Her arms were bare
And slim, and Tom Jerome, imagining
Them wrapped around him, smiled at his desire,
Then promptly threw all prudence in the fire
And joined the mourners gathered in a ring.
"*Buon giorno*," said Jerome. She turned her head
And saw the Ray-Bans and the smile . . . and fled!

6

She ran—perhaps a little wobbly—on
Those fabulous stiletto heels of hers.
(How likely was it that Louis Vuitton
Designed them for eluding murderers?)
But she had found a man whom she was faster than:
Jerome, who'd always thought himself a kindly gent,
Now wondering why she ran and what it meant.
Is it not strange, the way a woman can
Exactly find a place so inexact
As man's desire? In some it's just a craving for
Some morsel wrapped in an alluring dress.
But there is also this: the simple fact
That for a certain kind of man, there's nothing more
Alluring than a damsel in distress.

7

There was a poet who, enchanted by
A nightingale, had wished to follow him—
To fade, he said, "into the forest dim."
Who wouldn't want to merely sing and fly?
Jerome, who had a book of Keats nearby
Wherever he went (he used to take it to the gym—
He memorized the odes; the other stuff he'd skim),
Would read about that bird. *I can identify,*
He'd say. *An artist's life is so complex.*
So now appeared his bird, and all he yearned
For was to permanently lose himself
In song and soaring flight and—naturally—sex.
Good luck! No use in counting lessons learned,
Or why Keats called the bird "deceiving elf."

8

She led him, as they say, a merry chase,
Till, running short of breath, Jerome began
To think he might just die here in this place.
She'll wish someday she hadn't scorned the man
Who wasn't kidding when he said, "You know,
I'm dying just to meet you." Fierce remorse
Would then torment her; likely she would go
Become a nun; forsaking men, of course,
And mourning what she'd done. Such wicked bliss,
Imagining her melancholy search!
But no. Instead, she simply found a perch
And sat, her thighs crossed, with a cigarette. In this,
The Life of Tom Jerome, it's here he meets
Viña Fumento: at the grave of Keats.

9

"I'm not afraid of you," she fumed—she fumed!—
Nor would she turn her head. "My gracious," said
Jerome. "I'm hurt to think that you'd assumed
I'm dangerous. If so, you've been misled."
Said she, "If you are here to kill me, do
It, and if not, just go away." She had a knack
For smoking operatically. He said, "Could you
Spare me a cigarette? I need to buy a pack."
She found one in her bag. And now at last
He gazed on Viña's eyes. Renaissance
Eyes. Florentine hair. All Italy's past
Glories in her face. No use in faking nonchalance:
"Would you come dine with me? Who'd ever guess
That we'd have met like this, and here? Say yes."

10

"You are," she said, "a gangster sent to murder me!
You dress like all my husband's thugs. And you
Should lose the bad toupee." "I guarantee,"
Said he, affronted, "that I need no glue
To keep my hair attached. This pompadour
Takes time and care, and as for what I wear,
I bought this jacket on Rodeo Drive, though more
Or less a long time back. And let me spare
You any doubt regarding my intent.
I saw you at the funeral and said hello;
Next thing I know, I'm wondering where you went.
You're gorgeous; I make movies. And although
Both love and art are mostly in your head,
They're what I do. They're why I followed when you fled."

11

Audacious, that's the word for words like that;
She gave Jerome a reappraising glance.
Nor had he just been talking through his hat;
He was—had always been—a sucker for romance.
And she? Well, who could tell? Except that when
She spoke again it seemed a kind of settling in,
A look as if to say these games with men
Are always fun, so let this one begin.
"I should have known you are no gangster, you
Are so, so old! We two could dine, but I must see
If I can find you something soft to chew."
She laughed. And he? His every cell said, "I agree."
And what about her husband and his thugs?
Forgotten; lust is the champagne of drugs.

12

"*Risotto*, please, for *il signore,*" Viña said.
"Hilarious," he said. "I'll have the veal,
If just to prove I have some teeth left in my head."
"But who can tell," she said, "if they are real?"
Her very laughter could arouse him; she
Wore a perfume that unmanned him. "Do
You know," he murmured, "what you do to me?"
She said, "I'll bet you're married, aren't you?"
He raised his glass as if to give a toast.
"I'm single as of now, I'm pretty sure.
I have been married three times—four at most.
See? No amount of vexing exes seems to cure
This old proclivity of mine to make a mess.
Now just add wine . . . and you in that blue dress."

13

"You favor *moscardini*—baby octopi!"
"I do," said Viña, "Would you like to taste?"
Whereupon she fed him octopus; no need for haste,
As one hand held the fork, and one his thigh.
"Mmmm . . . maybe you are not," she whispered, "quite
So old as I had thought." "Do you," he asked, "regret
You stopped at graveside for a cigarette?"
"Do not make fun," she said. "Each day I have to fight
My fears, and find some courage here, inside."—
She took his hand and clasped it to her breast—
"You mustn't blame me that I run and hide.
If you'll but help me free myself, I'll do the rest."
Who could say no? "Today, I run away from home.
Tonight with you will be my last in Rome."

14

She brightened, just like that. "For me and you
It will be—how you say?—a piece of cake."
She fed him sweet (no teeth required!) tiramisu,
Suggesting airily that he should make
A movie here in Rome. He laughed: "The kind
Of indie movie I would do would cost
A million, maybe two. I guess I'll have to find
Some well-heeled widow eager to exhaust
Her fortune covering the cost." "Too bad,"
Said she, "I cannot be your lady financier
For I am neither rich nor widowed, sad
To say. But in his directorial career,
There's something any man can use,
A role that I can play: I'll be your muse."

15

This offer had a quick, predictable effect
Upon an aging fellow's vital signs.
No monitor with blinking lights and lines
Could ever, though, distinguish or detect
A symptom he had never known as yet:
A trembling in his scruples. Maybe wine's
The reason; sometimes alcohol inclines
A man toward revelations he'll regret.
But soon they left, and in the balmy dark,
On leafy streets, they climbed the Aventine Hill,
And from the terrace of a pretty park
They gazed across the Tiber, over Rome, until
She turned and simply kissed him. That's what Viña did;
And if he still had things to say, he kept them hid.

16

And so she brought him back to her hotel—
"A handsome relic from another time,"
She said, "like you." "Your wit has made the climb
Worthwhile," he said, "Just let me rest a spell
Inside, and if I fall asleep, then you can tell
Me later, really, it was quite sublime—
We loved like gods; and dastardly a crime
'Twould be if we should ever say farewell."
So how'd it go? They were, in fact, Olympian,
To judge by all the squeals and laughter it was clear,
And also, just to judge by every kiss.
"You are a flower," said Jerome, "Your skin
Is soft as petals, soft as petals here . . . and here . . .
And even . . . " "Shh"—she whispered—"Speak with this."

17

Jerome said, "You were born in Florence, I would guess."
She raised her head. "Why should I be from there?"
"Because the golden magic of your hair
Betrays you—like some Medici *comtesse*."
"It's true," she laughed. "I posed for Botticelli. Twice."
Said he, "You mock, but you're a flower, even so."
"I'm just an old corsage that has been put on ice
To keep it fresh. My husband likes to show
Me off. He spends a fortune doting on
My ripe old charms—this hair, these nails, this skin.
The azure dress that's lying on the floor? Milan.
But oh, you do not know the hell I'm in."
He brushed her forehead with his lips. "Old goat—
She said—"For that, I'll share a youthful anecdote."

18

"When I was fifteen, I was like a peach
That all the local fellows have to squeeze—
A peach that's dangling on the tree, and each
Competes to be the first to pluck it. Please, oh please,
My mama begged me—Viña, don't be weak!
But I knew sometimes weak is strong. And was I wrong?
A girl can have the world for just a song.
I told her so; she dragged me off to speak
With her physician. Such a kindly gentleman,
A gray and proper Swiss, so full of sound advice.
He reassured my mama, wished us luck, and then
At midnight called me on the phone. He'd sacrifice
His life for me—his work, his wife, and all he had.
So I ran off with him. I'm very bad."

19

With that, she laughed. Jerome did not ask how
The doctor ended up. Tonight what kept
His interest were two basic urges: more and now,
With grudging intermissions when they ate or slept.
In sum, his mind was disinclined to do the math
On whether risks are real, or great, or few;
What mattered was to wake and see her through
The open door, arising from her bath;
To watch her at the hallway closet, dripping, bare,
On tiptoe, reaching high up on a shelf
For—"*Ecco qui!*"—a favorite towel to wrap her hair.
He'd like to put this all in verse. But where
To find the words? What words could be the thing itself?
Nor does he wonder how she knew that towel was there.

20

Then came a knock. He called to Viña, "Sun's
Up! Time for coffee, lover," padded to
The door, and found a pair of thugs with guns
Were waiting for him there. The first one threw
Jerome against the wall; the second, quite
The cool one, struck a brooding gangster pose,
Then nonchalantly slapped him with his right.
He said, "Arkady, stuff some pantyhose
In this guy's mouth; but first we ought to know
His name. And that is—?" When Jerome replied,
The kid said, "Ah, you have a saint's name! So!
I guess you know the average saint, he died
A martyr. You, though, are about to lose your life
For screwing Viña—she's the Boss's wife."

21

Now Viña entered and surprised Jerome
By showing little in the way of fear.
"Oh, say it isn't you, Alfeo. Driving home
Will be so boring with you yacking in my ear."
Alfeo said, "And this old codger? Bet
You wore him out. Just looking at the bed,
I am surprised the old guy isn't dead,"
At which Arkady smiled and said, "Not yet."
Jerome, not so much frightened as confused,
Endured a pang of brokenheartedness.
The only thing he knew for sure was: He'd been used.
But used for what, and why, was anybody's guess.
"Dismayed?" Alfeo said, "I know just how you feel.
Now, if you would, just turn around—and kneel."

22

"Afraid not, pal," said Tom Jerome. "Forgive
Me, but this ain't the way that I intend,
When it arrives at last, to meet my end.
Just listen: Killing me is your prerogative.
But if you let me live—should I survive intact—
Then this could be your lucky break.
I'm sure you love the movies—you should act!
I've come to Italy with plans to make
A gangster flick. I'll need a leading man.
When my prospective backers ask me who
Should be the one, I'll tell them: You.
And there's a buddy role as well; who better than
Arkady here? You're on the road to fame and dough,
And all you have to do is let me go."

23

And yes, they bought it—in their leather jackets (one
With silver studs)—two promising movie stars
With guns, tattoos, and gang-related scars,
While Viña, laughing, said, "What have you done?"—
Already laying out her suitcase on the bed—
"You'll take a useful, homicidal hood,
And ruin him with dreams of Hollywood."
"You're one to talk of dreams and ruin, Viña," said
Jerome, relieved to be alive, but still.
She packed her things; Arkady went to fetch
The car; Alfeo leaned against the window sill
And turned his good side to the light. The wretch
Had put his faith in an absurdity;
But then, Jerome remembered, so had he.

24

Alas, she was the first one out the door,
And when he spoke and tried to catch her eye
She neither turned his way, nor said goodbye:
So much for words and deeds the night before!
Alfeo, on the other hand, gave him
The number for his cell. "I will await
Your call," he said—a kind of synonym,
Jerome assumed, for *better not be late.*
"Oh, sure, I'll call," Jerome replied. "The sky's
The limit, fellas. Your lack of any speck
Of talent, all the bogus gangsterisms—guys,
I gotta say I fed you all that movie dreck
Just so you wouldn't put a bullet in my head."
"Oh, really? Call me anyway," Alfeo said.

25

So now, appearing solo in that hotel suite:
A fellow in the aging Al Pacino mold,
Left feeling impotent and obsolete,
Bereft and cast aside—but mostly, old.
Was everything that Viña told Jerome
A lie? Just lines in an Italian play
In which the wife routinely runs away,
Enjoys her little outing, and is chauffeured home?
But what if this were so? It only meant
That she was doing what he'd often done:
With nothing but his guile, beguile someone.
It was, in fact, a kind of compliment,
Though this one felt so odd, so fade-to-black.
If only for a while, he thought, *I want her back.*

PART II

26

Downstairs, out on the gravel drive, he smoked
A cigarette the bellman gave him. "Geez, what day
Is it?" Jerome inquired. The bellman poked
His shoulder and exclaimed, "*Marone!* I'd say,
Signore, you are one disheveled guest.
Can you reveal the wicked woman who
Did such a thorough job on you?" "I'll test
Your memory," said Jerome, "A dazzler all in blue,
Who's likely brought a man to this hotel
A time or two." Again the bellman said, "*Marone!*"
But shook his head, and in a darker tone
He said, "Goodbye, my friend. I wish you well,
And pray you have a plan for what to do
When Cesare Fumento catches up with you."

27

"I need a taxi," said Jerome. "I'll say you do,"
The bellman sighed, "But no can do today.
For reasons known to none—or just a few—
All Italy's on strike. You'll have to make your way
On foot. The good news is Testaccio,
Though not the most attractive part of town,
Is only down the hill. You haven't far to go."
"Except," said groggy Tom Jerome, "which way is down?"
But off he went, just pleased that he could walk.
He liked the breeze. He knew he could have spent
The morning on the floor, outlined in chalk
By the authorities. This insight lent
A certain lightness to his step, but still he knew
He hadn't any inkling what to do.

28

No matter, though, how plaintively one's soul
Cries out for answers if it's time for lunch.
And yes, there's consolation in the crunch
Of a *panino,* and perhaps a bowl
Of *zuppa,* and a glass or two of wine.
Testaccio may lack the Aventine's
Arboreal grace, but it was rather fine
Here on the sidewalk, and, in fact, a lot like Queens:
A slice of pizza with your pals; a swirl
Of custard on a cone; a neighborhood
Of little shops and bars, your father's candy store;
Of nights out on the street; on lucky nights, a girl.
Now, all of this—this ordinary life—was good.
Yet somehow he required *something more.*

29

Try telling friends you need, well, *something more.*
They'll say, "Come on, what are you getting at?"
"It's just," he'd tell them, "Everything's a bore."
"That's all?" they'd laugh. "Cocaine's the cure for that!"
But what he really felt, he couldn't share:
That never, in the truest sense,
Had he experienced experience;
He'd rarely felt that he was really there.
And yet, just yesterday, he had. So now he set
Himself before the grave where he and Viña'd met.
"You wrote"—he said to Keats—"'La belle dame sans merci
Hath thee in thrall!' Was that addressed to me?
It must have been; it's what a poem is for—
Add poetry to flesh and you get *something more.*"

30

The early evening found him in his flat, alone,
While Viña in his mind made, as *la belle*
Dame sans merci had made, "sweet moan."
He reached across the pillows for his cell.
"Alfeo! Tom Jerome! I thought we might
Discuss this movie I'm about to make,
And work the kind of deal it's gonna take
To get us to L.A. on Oscar night."
He thought: *Good thing this little creep can't see*
I'm sitting in my skivvies on a bed
Where self-respecting bedbugs wouldn't be
Caught dead. "Yes, we should meet," Alfeo said,
"And good you called. I was about to launch a search.
I'd hate to think you'd left me in the lurch."

31

"You kidding? I would let this project go kaput
And hop the next flight back to Tinseltown
Before I'd think to shoot a single foot
Of film without you and that sexy frown.
Why don't you tell me where you'd like to meet?"
Alfeo said, "I know a restaurant
I think you'll find is just the thing. I'll greet
You out in front at ten. Of course, you'll want
To dress for dinner—you've a tux, I hope?"
Jerome said, "Nope." Alfeo sighed, "I could have lied
And said your jeans will do. But you could be the Pope
And not get in without a tux—he's tried."
"Oh," asked Jerome, "did Viña make it home all right?"
Alfeo laughed, "You'll see. Just wear a tux tonight."

32

Jerome was worried that he'd have to mount
A search. But finding a good tailor wasn't hard
And this one, bless his soul, took MasterCard.
He dressed Jerome like an Italian count.
Remembering the cabs were out on strike,
Jerome beseeched the tailor, while he changed
His clothes, to let him use his motorbike.
The tailor's smile was priceless: 'Twas arranged.
Jerome, in tux and Ray-Bans, made his way
Among the Vespas on the Lungotevere.
And feeling, well, Marcello Mastroianni-like,
He thanked the gods of mischief for the taxi strike.
The Tiber gleamed; the Roman traffic roared;
His heart—that rickety contraption—soared.

33

The kid, though, had been cagey when it came
To telling him *il ristorante*'s name.
"You mean I'm just supposed to guess? But how?"
"Relax. You'll know it when you see it. Ciao!"
He'd given him the number and the street,
But that was it. "This place is so discreet,
There's just a small brass sign, a single word
That would be meaningless unless you'd heard
Of it. The privileged few! Soon you'll be one,
And you'll be quite surprised before you're done."
Surprised? Well, yes and no, considering
The rather noirish rightness of the thing:
A sign that just said *VIÑA*—nothing more,
And everybody's favorite thug outside the door.

34

Alfeo, drowsy as a crocodile,
Bestirred himself and said, "I must confess
You look quite edible in evening dress."
And pouring on the charm, Sicilian-style,
Revealed a brilliant—if reptilian—smile.
The street was dark and this was Mack the Knife;
But Tom Jerome was thinking, *What's my life,*
That I should clutch it to me like a vial
Of nitroglycerin? If it should blow,
Then I'll have lived a bit before I go.
He made his way inside. A smile curled
As subtly as a wisp of smoke across his face,
Because his thoughts, on entering this place,
Were movie thoughts. He murmured, "In a world . . . "

35

A world, that is, of billionaires, of men whose lives
Are chronicles of power and prestige,
The kind whose vassals used to call "my liege."
This restaurant is where they take their wives,
Who get an evening out, a string of pearls
To say they're still desired, after all;
While through the forest frescoed on the wall
Immortal gods pursue the local girls.
These moguls would pursue the hostess here,
Except they know that chasing Viña might
Mean getting murdered in the dark one night.
They say, "How nice you look this evening, dear."
These men are rich, but each is just a man.
The gods in frescoes cannot die; *they* can.

36

And now here's Viña, mingling with her friends.
The regulars receive two kisses in the air;
And while they're dining, waiters bring a chair
For her to stop and chat; another table sends
Another bottle of prosecco; she
Admires the way a woman's had her hair
Done, then it's "just us girls": The two compare
And praise their perfumes, makeup, jewelry.
Of course, it's all a mere kabuki dance
Performed to let the husband know the wife
Knows hubby—craving Viña—has no chance.
The wife is happy, for this restaurant's
The only place in his triumphant life
She sees him fail to get the thing he wants.

37

. . . while at the bar the lone American
Is drinking on the house (it's Stoli, rocks).
There's always been a part of him that mocks
The rich but makes exceptions when
The drinks are free. But what is this abrupt
Disruption, something like a sonic boom
Made human? Cesare is in the room.
The Big Man says, "Don't let me interrupt,"
But none complain; not if they love their lives.
He says to Tom Jerome, "So you're the guy.
So you're the movie guy!" then pauses, and contrives
So frankly murderous a cast of eye
As would have anybody fearing for his life.
"You fuck my wife?" he says, "You fuck my wife?"

38

Which should be scary; but it's kind of wonderful.
Jerome, delighted, almost rubs his eyes;
He's just been tickled by a wild surmise:
"De Niro, right? You're doing *Raging Bull*!"
And Cesare, now all aglow, shouts, "So!
You *are* a movie guy! My boy here tells
Me you make better films than Orson Welles.
Can this be true? There must be much to know
About a man like you. Let's go inside
And have some dinner; after you've been plied
With pleasures you will never find at home,
You'll realize you've got a friend in Rome,
Which can be useful here if things get rough.
It happens. Not to worry: I'm a movie buff."

39

He looked like Pavarotti with those oiled curls,
A bear but for a pair of rather dainty legs.
He had a couple of Ukrainian girls
With breasts as big as ostrich eggs.
When he would—wordlessly—extend a hand
Behind him, they would—purring—fill his glass
Again. "They know what I am drinking, and
They always know what I am thinking." "Ass,"
Alfeo muttered. "Listen, movie star,"
The Big Man said, "You're hardly qualified to speak
About the women men are apt to seek.
When Tom and I are done with dinner, fetch the car."
Alfeo skulked away. The Big Man shook his head.
"That kid has got a lean and hungry look," he said.

40

The maître d' came by. "Your table, sir,
Awaits you." "Bravo! Rome was incomplete
Until I gave the town a place to eat.
Come on, my friend. Let's go create a stir."
They did, descending from the bar, the buzz
Of conversation spreading like a plume
Of expectation through the dining room.
Jerome thought, *Gracious, reputation does
A lot!* Just shaking hands with Cesare
Gives dining out a scandalous cachet
For guests who, even in their evening dress,
Must feel they've gotten boring; now they feel it less.
But look: An old man dressed in brown and red
Is watching them, then turns away his head.

41

In MGM days, Irving Thalberg would
Have made a call to central casting. They'd
Have found him someone with a face that could
Do just what this one did: Make you afraid.
The wolfish eyes that caught Jerome's just then
Unsettled him—they made him feel like prey.
He wouldn't want to feel that way again.
"A capo, now retired," said Cesare.
"He dines for free because he knew me when,
And can be trusted with the things he's seen.
In Sicily they have been making men
Like that one since the time of Constantine."
Jerome was thinking, but chose not to say,
He must have something on you, Cesare.

42

Jerome could only guess what vivid misery
Had once unfolded here, inside this ancient space.
"All Rome is fashioned from the rough debris
Created by mortality's embrace."
"And who said that?" he asked of Cesare.
"Well, I did," he replied. "You look surprised."
Jerome said, "Only that you have this way
Of keeping certain qualities disguised."
"As do we all." He formed an enigmatic smile.
"Nine-tenths of what you ever see is style.
Successful men all know you don't get far
Revealing who it is you really are."
A subtle test, perhaps? A certain cautious tact
Kept Tom Jerome from saying, "That's a fact."

43

"This dining room," he said, "just knocks me out;
A place that Bogey might have wandered through
At Warners', back in nineteen-forty-two."
"Well said," the Boss replied. "This place is all about
Theatrics. Guests of ours are in a kind of play,
Or maybe—as you say—a film we've made
In which they get to star. Our stock-in-trade
Is dreams and glamour. They are glad to pay.
And by the way, this evening we will dine
On steak. A steak puts lightning in your cock.
So it'll be *bistecca,* rare, and lots of wine—
Who knows when opportunity will knock?"
Jerome was at a loss for words. Just then,
The woman wearing blue appeared again.

44

No, not the same dress she was wearing when
They'd met—the one he'd helped her, in some haste,
To shed. Her husband puts his hand about her waist
And says, "At last . . . you meet again."
Jerome can feel his heart awake. It beats
Like choppy water. But of course, he's on "the foam
Of perilous seas," where a lover greets
A lover in *The Life of Tom Jerome.*
Aw, come on, Viña—that's him thinking—*slip*
A guy a sign! What would he have her say?
Perhaps she reads his mind; she shifts her hip
So that her husband takes his hand away.
"Well, certainly," says she, "we've met before—
What woman could forget that pompadour?"

45

Some chitchat followed, while the man she'd wed
Observed; no telling what was in his head.
"It seems to me that you have clientele
To greet. Go do the thing you do so well,
My sweet." That's what he said, but as she went,
His face said something rather different.
"Just look at her. The packaging's superb.
They have the power, like some magic herb,
To fuck you up no end. So let me share
A word of counsel, my new friend: Beware."
"Of Viña?" laughed Jerome. "You don't think I—"
"Forget it, Tom. It isn't worth a lie,
Although the one you told Alfeo was inspired.
Believing that one nearly got him fired."

46

"You think," said Tom Jerome, "that I'd deceive
Your boy with empty promises, and just
Because he gave me reason to believe
He was about to grind me into dust?"
The Big Man laughed: "And is it much to ask
A couple of my staff to go and fetch
My wife, and while they're at it, school the wretch
Who might've wrecked my life? How hard a task
Is that? But seriously, how's your steak?"
"The steak? It's great, though there's a question I've
Been pondering with each delicious bite.
For all your hospitality tonight,
I have to wonder why I'm still alive."
"Because," said Cesare, "we've got a film to make."

47

Now, that's the kind of moment when you want
To turn and give the audience a wink.
I smell good fortune in this restaurant.
And have a chance to hit it big, you think.
"So this is why your 'staff' arranged that I
Come here tonight, appropriately attired
For business with the Boss. And also why,
Although Alfeo let me off, he wasn't fired."
"All true. Just tell him you need actors and
He'll put that gun of his back on the shelf.
He's got ambitions that I understand;
I've dabbled in the cinema myself.
He wants to act. I, too, can be of use.
While you direct my picture, I'll produce."

48

"A kindly offer, but I'm not a one
To just say yes—though, yes, it might be fun."
"Ah, fun," the Big Man said, "is not as good
As making lots of money: Understood."
"And yet, you've done this kind of thing before,"
Jerome said. "Turned a profit? Tell me more."
"A little," said the Boss, "but still it seems
One can't accomplish everything one dreams
Of doing when the cast is only good
At screwing. I'm an artist who has borne
The bitter taste of cheap success." "I would
Assume," Jerome said, "what you make is porn."
"Indeed. But it's a toilsome task, producing trash.
Come help me make some art. I pay in cash."

49

"All right, then, tell me: Just what kind
Of movie do you have in mind?"
"It's more a feeling than a plan,"
Said Cesare, "I need a man
To put a feeling on the screen,
To make my unseen feeling seen.
But listen, we've both had enough
Of movie talk tonight. The stuff
That I have got in store for you
Will make you think you're twenty-two.
So come. It's time to seal the deal:
We've met, we've talked, we've shared a meal.
I've promised you that you'll get paid.
There's one thing left: Let's go get laid."

50

. . . at which, in rather an ebullient state,
He left to make a necessary call,
Which left Jerome alone to contemplate
The woodland scene depicted on the wall.
To watch a god pursue a shepherdess,
You'd think he'd have it all his way, and yet,
It's just a case of neverendingness:
The god's as close as he will ever get.
But me, I can still postulate success,
Believe in love, and not equivocate
About a woman in an azure dress.
At any rate, I'm in, and it's too late
To "fade away into the forest dim."
And that's when Viña reappeared to him.

51

How gaily did she drop into the chair
Beside him, bend so close he felt her breath
Caress his ear. He could have swooned to death.
"I've searched for you," she whispered, "everywhere."
"And yet," he muttered in reply, "you left me there,
Bereft. I even told your hired tough
That I had conned him with that movie stuff.
That might have been the end of me. I didn't care."
She laughed—but then, the room was full of eyes.
Her own were filled with feeling to the brim,
And seemed to search the soul inside of him.
"I had no choice," she said, "but to disguise
My feelings then. What if those thugs should see
What doing harm to you would do to me!"

52

The lights were dimming; it was after two.
The string quartet had left, and now a few
Departing guests were doing what they could
To catch her eye—all hoping that she might
Drop by before they left, and make their night.
"I have to go," she said. "This neighborhood
Is dangerous for lovers." "But I came,"
He said. "I had to see you, all the same.
Now, if you really mean to run away,
And you can swear to me the spell endures,
Then yes, we'll rendezvous today."
"I do. I can," she said, "I'm yours.
Palazzo Barberini has a garden where
We won't be seen. I'll meet you there."

53

She rose. He watched. "She really has the knack,"
Alfeo said, "for making people feel
Her shit is real." Jerome said: "So—you're back."
"That's right. I'm back. And what about our deal?
You know, the bait you dangle like a charm
Until you meet the Boss, and in a flash
Discard. You think I'm from the farm?
I know your game. He is a cow of cash.
Why do you laugh?" "Forgive me, kid. Some things
Don't easily convey. We say cash cow.
And—by the way—where is he, anyhow?"
"Right now? He's gone and left us underlings
To drive you to his club. It isn't far.
We'll talk a little business in the car."

54

Come on now, talk of business when you know
That through the window's Via Veneto?
La Dolce Vita swirled inside his head.
("Still, it's rather dull here now," Alfeo said.)
Fellini made the movie on this street,
Where, for the glitterati, life was sweet,
Though rotten underneath the skin. *But oh, the skin,*
Jerome was thinking. *Oh, the skin, the skin.*
A film in which he'd seen Anita Ekberg wade
Around the Trevi Fountain . . . what a splash she made!
Appealing to those parts of our identity
We had when first we climbed from out the sea.
"But now," Alfeo said, "it's time to talk. And when
We do, you'd best not lie to me again."

55

In truth, the Veneto was awfully dark
Compared with half a century ago.
"I'm telling you, Alfeo, let's just park
The car and kill him. Nobody would know."—
This from Arkady, sitting in the back,
Uncomfortably close if you were Tom
Jerome, who sensed in him a certain lack
Of zeal for making friends. Alfeo, calm
And cool as the Italian movie star
He wished he were, said, "Gee, it truly sucks
To get garroted in some gangster's car."
"And worse," Jerome laughed, "in a rented tux!
But why the fuss? We get along okay.
You think that I would lie to you? No way."

56

Such atmospherics in the Boss's car . . .
The darkness and the hour, the cigarettes,
As if the later in the night it gets,
The closer to some reckoning you are.
So then Alfeo said, "My cousin Ray
Has got a buddy in Los Angeles
Who's 'Dealer to the Stars.' We spoke today.
The facts regarding Tom Jerome are these:
You are a one-time moviemaker, yes,
But one who's so completely yesterday,
Your whereabouts are anybody's guess."
He added—like a cat with a canary-bird—
A beaming grin and said, "I must confess
It's fun to tell you this." And like the cat, he purred.

57

"Then damn, I guess this evens up the score,"
Jerome said. "Now you can inform your boss
You've saved him from a big financial loss."
To which the kid replied, "But wait! There's more!
And not just that you slept with the Madame
(Most everybody has who's had the chance),
But that you came to Rome because you're on the lam,
Then got the Boss to buy your song and dance.
You aren't just a failed director, but a thief.
And he will not be happy with your sham
Attempt to coax him past his disbelief
And dream of doing something really fine.
You would have brought his boyish hopes to grief.
It's what you do; it's what you did with mine."

58

Jerome said, "Kid, I disrespected you.
And if you mean to tell your boss the sum
Of what you've learned, well, maybe I would too.
But let me tell you where I'm coming from.
I'm thinking here's this guy who's got a deep
Appreciation for the finer things,
More suited to the company of kings
Than parking cars for some priapic creep.
What should you do? If I may be so brash,
Allow me to suggest that you stay mum
About my life. For Cesare's a cow of cash;
Let's you and I connive to get you some.
He thinks you're stupid and he pays you squat.
It's time you showed the SOB just what you've got."

59

At which point thugski mutters, "What the heck,"
And loops a cord around the old guy's neck.
He yanks it tight, so that with bulging eyes,
Jerome assumes that this is where he dies.
"Arkady!" cries Alfeo, "Let him go!
You're ruining our chance to make some dough!"
"Some dough?" the Russian says, "What kind of dunce
Would let him fool you twice? He fooled you once."
But grudgingly, Arkady lets the old guy drop.
He shakes his head: "You just got lucky, Pop."
Jerome, who, following this brush with death,
Is trying both to speak and catch his breath,
Says, "Sudden strangling's kind of hard on me.
Could you two just agree to disagree?"

60

Alfeo lit Jerome a cigarette
And, laughing, said, "You are so full of shit.
To think that, for a while, I fell for it."
Jerome said, "Still, you let me live. I'm in your debt.
But listen, kid, don't tell your boss. The fact
Is, you're the one who hooked me up with him.
And though you never know how he'll react,
I think he'd want to tear you limb from limb."
"So your advice," Alfeo said, "is just to do
Whatever works out tidiest for you."
"No, what I'm saying is, play ball with me
And we will stick it to the man. You'll see.
It can be done, Alfeo, but we must
Rely on something unaccustomed: trust."

61

Now this, Jerome was thinking, this could blow
To kingdom come my fragile little plan.
As if it weren't half-assed to begin with, no?
But now the shit could really hit the fan.
And for a connoisseur of irony,
It's quite the feast, for all this juicy stuff
Alfeo thinks he's found is far from free
Of flaws. It's not quite true, but true enough
To do me in, and wreck the brand-new life
That I've been hoping to achieve by getting paid
To make a movie that would not be made
And running off with my producer's wife.
This kid can tell him that I'm full of shit,
But even so, he doesn't know the half of it.

PART III

PART III

62

"Well, look who's here—you're late! I would have thought
You all had robbed a bank and gotten caught!"
A merry man, this Cesare, who, roaring, rose
To greet them. He was sniffling, though. His nose
Was raw. Jerome knew well enough the way big rush
Can turn two healthy nostrils into mush.
Still, he was quite the vision, Cesare,
Resplendent in a caftan made of gold lamé:
A rajah, glowing under candlelight,
Amidst a harem's worth of ladies of the night,
All garbed in gauzy pants and nothing more,
Embodying what candlelight is for:
An alchemy Jerome knew well but couldn't name,
The warmer form of flesh their flesh became.

63

"Now this, my friend, is how Rome should be enjoyed:
Between the hours of two and six a.m.,
Among my pretty women, scads of them.
Are they not wonderful? And all employed
To love just you. They'll bend to kiss the hem
Of your pajamas, all these scrumptious, red-
Hot Eastern European mamas. None of them
Is into drama—pay the money, off to bed.
We train them, too, in all the whirls and twirls.
So be my guest, and pick out one or two.
We've even got some retro girls with curls
Between their legs, if that appeals to you."
Jerome said, "Gosh, it's just too hard to choose!"
To which the Boss said, "Tom, you can't refuse."

64

And yet he did, although reluctantly.
For while he valued few delights above
The pretty misses, like the number of
La belle dame's kisses, he had reasons three.
The first? His heart. He thought it best to spend
Whatever heartbeats he had left on love,
And not some gal some guy decides to shove
At him, on some intoxicated whim.
The second was his soul. He could pretend
It didn't matter, that these girls were pros.
But that would only make him one of those
Who lets the devil get the best of him.
And in the end, the one I want, you see,
Is Viña, only Viña. That was reason three.

65

"C'mon," said Cesare, "you can't say no to this.
It's party time! Don't blow an easy chance."
To which Jerome replied, "I can't dismiss
The thought there should be something in a kiss."
The Big Man laughed. "That's up to you! Let's dance!"
Jerome said, "Let me have my sedentary bliss."
This time the Big Man smiled, but did not laugh.
"Perhaps I need to hand you over to my staff.
Marone! We're known for fun, if you recall.
But what's a host to do? A potted plant's
More fun than you! Alfeo and Arkady, haul
His ass out on the floor!" They did. Then all
Those pretty women, slipping off their gauzy pants,
Converged like serpents at the serpents' ball.

66

Some hours passed. The merriment had ceased.
The Big Man, like an aerial balloon
From which the helium had been released,
Lay draped across a chair. His Russian goon,
Arkady, watched him snore, and with a bored contempt
He calculated where his interests lay—
Be loyal to the Big Man, or attempt
To play the hand he held another way.
But then Jerome came in to wake the Boss,
"Just so the day won't be a total loss."
He woke and mumbled, "Booze and drugs and sex—
We're like a pair of studio execs.
But let's get down to work. I've got a hunch
You've got a pitch to make me. Let's do lunch."

67

Whereupon he sent Arkady down the street
For Chinese food: "It's what producers eat."
He looked quite pleased. "I wanted us to dine
As if we were on Hollywood and Vine."
Jerome was tickled; ate his Hunan pork
Off a paper plate, with a plastic fork.
And meanwhile, from Alfeo, not a word
Regarding things about Jerome he'd heard,
Which left the old guy able to proceed
With conning Cesare, as they'd agreed.
"Let's make a film together," said Jerome,
"In which the setting is the finest joint in Rome:
Your restaurant, where glitterati come to know
La dolce vita 2.0."

68

"Fellini! Bravo!" Cesare enthused,
"Though next time I'd prefer you come equipped
With something more substantial, like a script."
"A script?" Jerome replied. "The master used
To carry the entire story in his head.
'I find that scripts are deadly things
That only bind the muse's wings.'
Unlikely though it seems, that's what he said."
The Big Man rumbled—then he blew: "Son of a bitch!"
He flung his platter full of Peking duck
Aside and said, "That's what you call a pitch?
You think l just fell off the turnip truck?
You think you'll merely wave a magic wand
And I'll believe that crap? I won't be conned!"

69

Jerome shrugged. Every film producer has
A mandatory tantrum once a day.
"All done? Now listen to me, Cesare—
Assuming that you're through. Last evening as
We dined at *Viña*, part of you—the tough-guy part—
Revealed a side that most don't get to see.
It's starved for truth and beauty, love and art—
A thing you've managed to conceal, but not from me.
So can I help you find the cinematic terms
In which to speak, before you're food for worms?
Of course, I can. The question's merely one of what
It is that drives you to pursue this thing.
Your business side may say it's money, but
That gangster soul of yours just yearns to sing."

70

"Tom, let's just can the sentimental stuff.
It's easy to believe, admiring some cutie
From behind, that beauty's truth, truth beauty.
But comes a time you say goodbye to youth,
And then you recognize that money's truth,
Truth money. That is all ye know on earth,
And for these girls, it's all their beauty's worth.
Now, as for love and art, I've seen enough
To know these two commodities have got
One trait in common—cost; they cost a lot.
Romance is an illusion and the source
Of heartache and ennui; while art, of course,
Gives clarity and comfort, which is why
I'd like to make a little art before I die . . .

71

. . . but Holy Mary, not if I must spend
And spend until it seems there'll be no end.
You've told me nothing but the best will do,
But I'm the one who'll write the checks, not you.
I've made a lot of films, and, Tom, my boy,
The folks involved are still in my employ.
You haven't, for example, seen the last
Of all my pretty women—they're your cast.
Your friend Alfeo, skulking by the door,
Has played the male lead for me before.
Of course, he's only acted with his dick.
With you directing, though, he'll catch on quick.
So I've got cast and crew; equipment too;
The only big expense I'll have is you."

72

"Well," said Jerome, "Here's some of what you get
By spending money on a man like me.
If all you've got as yet is just a feeling, let
Me let you in on a reality.
Regardless of the plot, or prettiness
Of 'pretty women' willing to perform
In ways that take the male id by storm,
We need a special woman in an azure dress.
Just look around: There isn't one of them
Who's got the fire to play the fatal femme.
You need the emblematic female, of a kind
A man could search the world and never find.
But damn if Viña—your own Viña—isn't she.
Your own dear wife! It's . . . serendipity."

PART IV

73

"So you were thinking," Viña said, "of me?
But they're so young, their tummies hard and flat.
Most men I know, they tend to go for that."
"My butterfly," he smiled, "the living clay
That is your flesh, the living silk your skin—
I do not care what shape your abs are in."
"Don't lie. A woman has to catch the eye
And cause some chaos in your nether parts.
Who really thinks that men love with their hearts?"
Said he, "You sound like Cesare some hours ago,
Deriding the idea of love. He said of this,
'You are just worshipping an orifice.'
And yet I wonder who he's trying to kid.
I think he's got some deeper feelings hid."

74

"Explain this word—this orifice—to me."
"I could, my butterfly, but I might risk
A little mangled Keats." She whispered, "Tsk,
It's just *la mia passerina!*" "No," said he,
"We mustn't call her it. We'll call her she.
She is my beaker full of the warm South,
She is the coming musk rose, a second mouth,
An essence, like an oyster, like the sea.
The secret—" "Shh," said Viña, "poetry
Cannot compete with this . . . and this . . . and this . . .
And if you keep on chattering you'll miss
This . . . and oh, this . . . and oh, and . . . there, you see?"
Of course, he saw. It's what a muse is for—
The poetry and flesh, the *something more.*

75

She ran her fingers down his cheek and said,
"I love your whiskers, darling. Never shave.
They make me crazy when you misbehave.
And oh, to think of all that lies ahead;
Let's always spend our afternoons in bed."
What bliss, what sense of *this is it* she gave
Him! Sure at last she loved him, he would save
Her from the empty glamour and the dread
She'd said her life with Cesare involved.
So now he told her: "We have cut a deal
To make a movie with an actress who
Has yet to act—and won't, in fact. It's you!
Instead, we'll take his money, put it toward our real
Intent, and run away together . . . problem solved."

76

Well, maybe, maybe not. For with a sigh
That begs deciphering, she turns her head
Away from him and rises from the bed.
He says, "You're happy, aren't you, butterfly?"
She's gazing down upon the garden where
They'd rendezvoused. He'd run through Rome to meet
Her there. He hears the traffic in the street.
The wind, as in the movies, lifts her hair.
In profile, standing there, she's Venus. One
Can only marvel: Wheatfields ripening in
The sun are not more golden than her skin.
He's thinking, *Stick a fork in me—I'm done.*
And now, she faces him: "How wonderful you are
To make your butterfly a movie star!"

77

"Viña, this thing that we've been working on
Is not some ordinary movie deal.
I hope you understand, it's just a con.
We're in it for your husband's cash; it isn't real."
"But you're a great director, don't you see?
Our love has led you to the financier
You had to find to make a movie here.
How could we waste this opportunity?"
But it occurred to him, what "we" implied:
A change of plans, but more, a change of heart.
He muttered only, "You'll be perfect for the part."
In this, *The Life of Tom Jerome,* the tide
Had crested: *Viña sees no need to run;*
She can remain in Rome and have her fun.

78

I like to think—he thought—I have a knack
That compensates for other skills I lack:
I tend to know what other people want.
Just take that moment at the restaurant
When hubby had some cautionary things to say
Behind her back as Viña walked away.
I knew—though he himself might well be unaware—
That he would sell his soul to keep her there.
He'd finance almost any movie, more or less;
Just make it all about his wife and he'd say yes.
Which, true to my astute analysis,
He did. But what about what Viña wanted? This,
I knew—I knew—was to escape somehow.
I would have bet my life on that . . . until just now.

79

"We'll go to Cannes!" she cried, "Pavilions full
Of paparazzi jostling for a shot!
Yours is old and mine is new, but two careers so hot,
They'll throw confetti at the festival.
Of me, they all will cry, 'A star is born!'
Of you, 'Jerome is back on top again'—
And ooh, I'll testify to that!" But then
She caught herself, and said, "Why so forlorn?"
Forlorn!—he thought—"*The very word is like a bell
To toll me back from thee . . .* " *At last I see
What, dazzled as I've been, I couldn't tell
Myself: Don't take her feelings personally.
In life and love, the dumbest thing you'll ever do
Is think the nightingale sings for you.*

80

His nightingale caught a taxi back
To *Ristorante Viña*. "I must show
Myself, or Cesare will blow his stack."
And Tom Jerome, well, he was pleased to know
The taxi strike was over. "Five'll get you ten,
My tailor's wondering if he'll ever see
That missing motorbike of his again.
Tonight he'll get it back. Then, as for me . . . "
Then, as for him? For him? Remarkably,
For all the brutal battering his dreams
Had taken, what he felt—and selflessly—
Was love. *She wants to be a star. It seems
I have a chance to make that happen. But
I'm like the dog who caught the car—now what?*

81

The question found its answer in his cells.
The conscious mind eternally insists—
As if it could—on knowing what impels
Our actions. But the cells do not make lists.
Suppose that, just this once, they did. The first
Things itemized would be: the withered loves
Of former wives; the wasted gifts; the thirst
For thrills, the drugs, the all-of-the-aboves.
But second—knowing he'd been waiting for a sign
By which to fend off the encroaching blues
And "burst Joy's grape against his palate fine"—
Was everything she'd done for him, as muse.
The truth is, she was born to play the part.
I'll make the film, and damn the broken heart.

82

Resolve is good. What he remembered now,
However? Countless tasks that needed doing. These
Included writing something. *Holy cow!*
It's not like scripts are falling from the trees!
But then it struck him, fleeing from the thought
Of sitting at the keyboard, overwrought:
Not every movie needs a script. It's wise
Sometimes to let your actors improvise.
With this consoling notion in his head,
He took a valium and went to bed,
When out of nowhere came the movie's final shot,
A coalescence out of nothingness—
Completely independent of the plot—
But it will make the movie, nonetheless.

PART V

83

"Midnight! Ah, the hour is propitious! Time
To scout locations for this work of art.
La mia Roma at its most lubricious! I'm
The man to lead you through it—let us start!"
So . . . think of Dante touring hell, beginning
To learn from Virgil what the dead endure.
But here it's Cesare as guide instead. He's spinning
A different take on sinning, that's for sure.
"Do people really think their Lord and Savior
Could give a damn about their bad behavior?
Two thousand years and still the myth persists
That someone up there judging you exists."
"I'd not," Jerome observed, "make light if I were you.
He's got you penciled in for circle number two."

84

They passed St. Mary of the Victory.
The Boss said, "Let us interrupt our search,
As there's this girl inside you've got to see.
The fetching Saint Teresa's in this church,
The subject of a certain notoriety,
As virgins are expected to be pure.
But she? A saint of sexual allure,
Or—shall we say—of saintly impropriety."
Jerome beheld Bernini's marble maid,
Enraptured by an angel's golden shaft.
"That is a tad unseemly, I'm afraid,"
He said, and then—in church, aloud—he laughed:
"My guess is, you'll have company in circle two.
But still, the chances you'll get laid in hell are few."

85

"Tom, here's the problem Dante Alighieri had.
He was a tight-ass member of the Catholic Church,
And thought that pleasure was, by definition, bad,
When pleasure's just one facet of the search
For spiritual meaning through a feeling
Of sexual catharsis, whether it's overt
Or not. See? Saint Teresa's face is quite revealing,
As if her visitation from an angel hurt,
But, as we say, hurt good. Now, does she get
To go to heaven? Should she burn in hell?
The author of *Inferno* couldn't, I would bet,
Though touched with rare poetic genius, tell."
Jerome concurred. "Who could pretend to guess?
All saints have holes, all sinners holiness."

86

To judge, though? Just a waste of thought. Beginning
At birth, we're wrought to want things. In a sense,
Not sinning is a greater sin than sinning;
What poet ever wrote in praise of abstinence?
Jerome was thinking of his boy, John Keats,
Who never made it with the girl next door—
O, Fanny Brawne!—among those grand conceits
Through which the poet glimpses *something more.*
Unlike the heedless Paolo and Francesca, they
Were bound by custom; didn't even try
To free themselves, until he sailed away
To Rome, to curse propriety, and die.
This bothered Tom Jerome, because the kid
Deserved to get the girl and never did.

87

It's nature's sense of humor: make you short
And hypersensitive, and make you poor.
Let Shakespeare's ghost, and Chapman's too, exhort
You into poetry, to reach for *something more*.
Then summon critics who are at their best
When smothering nightingales in the nest.
But meantime, make you scrappy, tough—the sort
Of kid who'll clap his thigh and get up off the floor
And write an ode or two. You cannot thwart
The operatic ending nature has in store,
But go, John Keats, go crush Joy's grape for all it's worth.
And know that when your body brings you back to earth,
"Beauty is truth, truth beauty" is your test
Of being. Death is your perfected birth.

88

At times he wondered why he got the days
The more deserving didn't; been so blessed
He even got the girl (although, in painful ways,
A girl who could be had but not possessed).
That said, he had decided some time back,
In lieu of passing judgment on
The Life of Tom Jerome, to cut himself some slack.
To every lover, every artist (even con),
Apply a pair of Keatsian reflections
The poet gleaned from grief and exaltation:
"I am certain of nothing but
        the holiness of the Heart's affections
And the truth of the Imagination."
In these a kind of grace is to be had.
So don't begrudge yourself the days. Be glad.

PART VI

Cary Grant
Myrna Loy

89

Scouting locations with a man who deals
In food and drink (plus varied forms of crime)
Means you'll be stopping frequently for meals
And meeting characters from time to time.
In Campo de' Fiori, who turned up
But Pio, dapper coffee bar habitué,
Who sipped *espressi doppi* by the cup,
While selling crystal meth for Cesare.
"This neighborhood!" he sighed. "I used to love the place.
But now at night the soccer thugs run wild.
They're like these aliens from outer space."
The Big Man patted Pio's hand and smiled.
"We're doing great. But—do I need to tell
A man like you?—don't dis the clientele."

90

That clientele, in loud, unruly throngs,
Runs wild through the piazza late that night.
Jerome observes them under vapor light.
It's Dante's seventh circle, but with soccer songs.
He tells his camera guy where he belongs,
Then checks his male stars. They're quite the sight,
Alfeo and his bud, the erstwhile Muscovite.
He tells them, "Skip the standard rights and wrongs
Of acting. Simply be the guy you play.
Now you, Alfeo, with your sexy stubble,
You've always had your way with girls—unless
It's Viña. Chase her as she runs away
And curse her as the source of all your trouble.
She vexes you, this woman in the azure dress."

91

Alfeo nods. His Russian friend, though, seems
So pleased to take direction from Jerome,
He smiles and shows his teeth. One tooth is chrome.
So even killers have their dreams.
"Well, look at you," Jerome says. "Menace, heft,
And now we've given you the wardrobe and the gloss
To play the kind of hood that other hoods call Boss.
A brief encounter with your wife is all that's left.
The woman running through the square? That's her,
So caught up in her lovers' quarrel, she doesn't know
You've been here, watching. She's about to go
From frying pan to fire, as it were."
"Oh, yeah?" Arkady says, "I'll fix that pretty whore.
There's not a man who'll want to chase her anymore."

92

"That's good!" said Tom Jerome. "I'm really thrilled!
Remember, though—I know you're fairly new—
No members of the cast need actually be killed.
We're movie-making; make-believe will do."
But this was only partly true. The thugs were real,
Their whistles and their groping hands. He planned to make
His leading lady run a gantlet, make her feel
She was in real-life danger for his movie's sake.
Arkady said, "She needs a thing to fear.
You want the girl to know real terror here.
You think the Boss's wife can't act, and I agree.
But she won't need to act when she runs into me."
At which the Big Man, overhearing, said,
"You're out, you shit. I'll play the part instead."

93

The Russian, measuring his choices, says, "Yo,
There goes a promising career. But as they say,
The one who's called 'the money' runs the show."
Jerome thought, *Whoa, this just might be okay:*
Who better in the role of Cesare,
Than Cesare? And what—more chaos? So
Much the better, no? It's cinéma vérité!
When Viña sees it's Cesare, you never know,
The moment might just get us where we want to go:
That single frame at which to point and say,
'That's her! That's her! That's all ye need to know.'
"Jerome," he heard Alfeo mutter, "Way
To go. 'No film,' you said, 'We'll merely bilk the man.'
So now, of course, he's starring in the thing. Good plan."

94

"C'mon, it only means he's bought it, kid.
You wondered if he'd pay for all of this. He did.
So think nice thoughts. What more assurance could you want
Than this: Right now, they're readying the restaurant
Where we'll be shooting in a day or two,
And there'll be opportunities for me and you
To dip our fingers in the cookie jar.
It isn't whether, but how much, how far
We can induce him to extend this bash.
He is, as you'll recall, the cow of cash,
Who has been calculating from the start
The ROI of putting money into art.
He only thinks he's smart. I know what makes him tick.
It's love, not money. This you'll learn, and quick."

95

O, horn of plenty for the male eye!
Emerging, like the great Italian ladies
Of decades long gone, from a black Mercedes,
Viña provides the briefest glimpse of thigh,
And raises pandemonium thereby.
Alarmed, Jerome is suddenly afraid he's
Arranged for Proserpine to visit Hades:
His plan to send her through this crowd could go awry.
But Viña laughs it off: "What thug would mess
With me in this fantastic azure dress?
I'll tell them what I'd say to hoodlums anywhere:
I'll claw their eyes out if they touch my hair.
I'll run in heels on cobblestones and brave a mob
To make this film. I am an actress. It's my job."

96

All morning, flower vendors set the tone—
The sun, the tourists. But on weekend nights,
This square is ruled by swarms of social parasites.
The bravest women will not walk alone,
But Viña will. She'll be herself and start
A noisy lovers' quarrel, then take flight,
All for the rare, contrarian delight
Of breaking yet another male heart.
In fiction or in fact, though, it's a risky path,
This heedless weaving through the world of men.
She's loved and run away before, and will again.
The problem here is, costs accrue—it's only math—
And living so capriciously is tough to do.
She only thinks she's tough enough, he knew.

97

Now Viña, racing through the crowded square,
Is followed by a hand-held camera crew
(a popular technique from their
Director's youth, when Nouvelle Vague was new.)
He'd said, "We'll film in shaky black and white,
The better to convey her point of view.
More threatening than tender is the night;
The lens will capture what she's going through.
We've got our damsel in distress, all right,
Enduring all the crude abuse, the cruel laughter.
Might she be rattled just a little bit? She might.
The real test, though, will come thereafter."
Oddly—odd, indeed—Jerome has failed to say
That waiting at her gantlet's end is Cesare.

98

At dawn, she lay with her director, spent
From her exertions of the previous night,
Her body the superb embodiment
Of what the poet called *enwreathed light*.
But light is unreliable when wrapped
In flesh, so here the art of film is apt,
Which holds the light in ways that bodies can't.
Just think of Myrna Loy or Cary Grant;
Conventionally dead, onscreen they give
The lie to death. Onscreen they live.
They live as in a waking dream, as do—
When all is nearly said and done—we two.
He told her all of this. "My sweet old boy,"
She said. "It may be so, but who is Myrna Loy?"

99

"My lovely Viña, all this fine romancing
Is tangling up my truant disposition.
This and your husband's generous financing
Have steered me toward a loftier ambition.
Time was, I wanted just to make a buck,
But then I wanted more, to be the portal
To your freedom. But now I'm truly stuck:
I long to render you, my love, immortal.
But who am I to do it? Film directors must,
To spin the magic that a good one makes,
Apply a certain quantity of fairy dust;
I lack the fundamentals that it takes.
I lack the genius and the craft."
At which his Viña rolled her eyes, and laughed.

100

"You speak—is this the word?—rhetorically,
When you declare that actors live forever.
Perhaps they do, but only metaphorically.
It's not the same as this"—she touched him—"Ever.
I haven't any interest in the spirit,
Or in inhabiting some waking dream.
And as for dying, *caro*, do not fear it;
It's not so scary as they make it seem.
Just make a movie to delight the living,
And if it blows up in our faces, say
You're sorry; I for one, am quite forgiving.
(Though who would say the same for Cesare!)
So hush, I'm in your corner, full of trust
That you will find that quantity of fairy dust."

101

Next day, arriving at the restaurant,
He found the makeup guy, the wardrobe guy,
The lighting guy, the guys who did the sound,
The slew of extras who'd been standing by.
"It's time we got this rocket off the ground,"
He told them. "All you've got—that's all I want."
He had those Ray-Bans and that pompadour,
An empathetic way with crew and actors,
The Al Pacino charm and other factors
That won their trust and confidence. What's more,
Alfeo, not so trusty heretofore,
Was keeping mum about Jerome's detractors.
It's not the time for ditching benefactors,
He'd decided, not with wealth and fame in store.

102

Arches and alcoves, the inescapable
Inference that the dead are never gone,
That human ingenuity is capable
Of works and words through which the dead live on.
"It's Rome," said Cesare. "He found a kernel
Of truth, the guy who dubbed this town eternal.
This space, which has been used a thousand ways,
Now breathes the residue of ancient days
When Thracian slaves were sheltered in its walls,
And Caesar's horses curried in their stalls.
One day a place where cows were butchered, next day home
To pampered nobles—as I said, it's Rome—
And finally a playground where the privileged could
Relive the glamour, not of Rome, but Hollywood."

103

So here, with kilograms of golden bling
About his jowly neck, the Boss is sharing know-
it-all-advice on every little thing.
Jerome's okay with that: "We're good to go.
And these pornographers of yours—they've bruised
Their youthful dreams a little, making do
With making films in which their talents weren't used—
But now they're all afire, and all because of you,
Who said, 'Let's put a feeling on the screen,'
And left it up to me—and them—to read
Your heart's intent and make that feeling seen.
Let's give them room to do their thing. Agreed?"
"Agreed," said Cesare. "No more demands save one.
You've got three days to shoot. And then we're done."

104

Behind the bar, in Viña's dressing room,
The star had made a nonnegotiable demand.
"I can't perform without my Baccarat perfume.
Am I supposed to wear just any brand?"
Jerome knew well what magic draws us in;
It's in the actor's mind and heart, and on her skin.
And though the camera cannot film a smell,
When actors lack the magic, you can tell.
So he conveyed all this to Cesare, who winced
At the expense, but knowing Viña, was convinced.
He glanced across the set for anybody
With nothing much to do. "Hey, you! Arkady!
Go find and fetch us *la signora*'s scent."
The Russian gave a hooded stare, but out he went . . .

105

. . . and back he came, with perfume in that pyramid-
Shaped bottle, though needing to be reimbursed
A thousand euros for it when he did.
The Big Man taunted him a little first:
"Our errand guy! We've found our errand guy,
Who gave—however briefly—playing me a try,
But doesn't let the yen to act consume
Him when he's told to fetch the star's perfume."
That said, as if on cue the star herself came out,
And sure enough, she cast that magic glow about.
The men all knew, just looking at her face,
The perfume met with Viña's satisfaction,
So that, with everything and everyone in place,
Jerome could soon announce, "Lights! Camera! Action!"

106

"Do you recall, *ragazzi*, what occurred
Out on the square a couple nights ago?
Now, whether you were there or merely heard,
You must pretend you don't already know.
For what we shot was our concluding scene,
And what we shoot today we shoot as though
The things already shot had not yet been,
Which is to say, we've got a ways to go.
In real life love affairs, we can't conceive
Of what will happen next, or how, or why.
But as practitioners of make believe,
We chart the arc that love will take—or try."
This from Jerome, the rare director who pretends
He doesn't know just how the story ends.

107

The camera carries this director's hopes
Of capturing the moment when the sparks
Begin to fly between a pair of sharks—
How sleek they are!—who claim that love's for dopes.
But this is one of nature's oldest tropes:
The disbelievers are the easiest marks,
A rule that's fueled a million story arcs
Depicting the inevitable slippery slopes.
"Hey, Marco!" says Jerome. "If any cameraman
Can catch the sparks in flight, you can."
And Marco, an Italian, shouts, "Just give me light!
I'll fashion poetry in black and white!"
Hah! Keats and Dante had the gift of verse.
I've got an old pornographer. Things could be worse.

108

"For ten years," said the Boss, "he's worked for me,
And never once has Marco mentioned poetry.
The same with Rafi, who has never found,
So far as I'm aware, his bliss recording sound.
Apparently my people feel"—and here he laughed—
"A sacred obligation to their craft,
Which, much to my chagrin, I'm forced to say,
I'd somehow overlooked until today.
What is it, Tom Jerome, that lets you see
In everyone a germ of possibility?
You're like a wizard or an old savant
Who has the gift of knowing just what people want.
It must—to watch you with our merry elves—
Consist of letting people be themselves."

109

Jerome said, "Kid, you enter and assume
A pose atop the stairway leading down
To where the hostess in the azure gown
Is wowing patrons in the dining room.
She's doing what she does—which is enhance,
For those who lack her natural noblesse,
Despite their wealth, or how they dress,
The dream of finding passionate romance.
But now it's she who dreams it. Look at you:
You're sexy and you're dangerous! She itches
After you, as women did Alain Delon.
Now you must show us you're attracted too.
You've feigned enthusiasm with your britches
Off, but now you have to fake it with them on."

110

There on the landing by the bar he stood.
The tux, the tats, the gang-related scars,
Straight out of gangster films he was, or noirs:
The kid who'd managed to escape the neighborhood
And sworn he'd make it to the top. He would.
Not long ago, his job was parking cars.
But now the big shots with their fat cigars,
They watch him warily—and well they should.
Those pricey molls of theirs are watching too,
Aware of sudden currents running through them.
He plays the part that movie stars are for:
To populate your dreams as if your dreams were true.
That's always been the way that people view them—
As near as they can get to *something more*.

111

"We've missed you at the club these past few weeks!
Alfeo tells me you've been working hard
At tightening that screenplay till it squeaks.
But still, you might be prudent to regard
Said screenplay as a draft until I've made some tweaks.
Let's call it pride of place. I've paid and Viña's starred—
So, Tom, I get to say okay before she speaks.
If not, well, I would hate to play the money card."
"Oh, never!" laughed Jerome, who did not fear
That Cesare would ruin what he'd written,
Because there was no script—no, not a word thereof.
By night he wasn't at his desk, but here
In Viña's arms, still bittersweetly smitten.
He had more urgent things to do—for love is love.

112

And talent's talent. Marco had a thought:
"Instead of just connecting dots, why not devise
An entrée into Viña's mind? What taught
Her heart to be so hard? Let's improvise
The perfect cinematic shot, or near it—
The moment when the character she's playing spies
Alfeo, shakes her head as if to clear it.
A lock of hair drops fetchingly across her eyes.
The screen is momentarily obscured,
Which gives us opportunity to mask
A little sleight of hand. You give the word—
The cast and crew will set about the task."
Jerome just beamed. It was as if a gust
Of wind had carried in some fairy dust.

113

So Marco drained another *doppio*
And said, "We'll do a series of dissolves—
No reams of words required—with which we'll show
What Viña's marriage to the Boss involves.
(Not Viña—heavens, no!—the character she plays.)
It's *Beauty and the Beast*, except no handsome prince
Appeared, for all this wife's obliging ways,
And so her heart's grown harder ever since."
"That's brilliant!" said Jerome. "We'll capture how—
Through closeups of their hands and faces—
They've moved from near to far apart, till now
They've stashed their dreams in hidden places."
"Of course!" cried Marco, "Hands and eyes, you know!
Their hands and eyes are all we need to show."

114

And off he went, which left Jerome
Enduring something of an awkward pause
In which Alfeo, brooding, pushed the foam
Around his cappuccino. And the cause
Of his preoccupation? "Hands and eyes,"
He said. "'Show hands and eyes!' I'm just a cog.
I'm not an actor. All your promises were lies.
I haven't been assigned a line of dialogue!"
Jerome, bemused, beheld the boy. "I guess
You think you simply aren't cool enough
To mesmerize the woman in the azure dress
Unless you say a lot of words and stuff.
But you're more likely with the way you walk
And look to win her than with fancy talk . . .

115

. . . or *any* talk. Young protégé of mine,
You think we measure out a role like twine?
Recall, it's your charisma that this shot
Is all about, so use that thing you've got.
A great director told me never to
Write dialogue when images will do.
The same for actors who rely on words;
They're tethered to the earth like flightless birds.
The better ones can prompt a wild surmise
Without a word, and so we watch their eyes.
That said, of course, they're creatures of their glands,
And so we also need to watch their hands.
Now go. Show Marco's lens the love and violence
That lurk behind the tux and tats—and silence."

PART VII

116

Marco said, "Tom, meet Amber. Amber's got
A derriere that's perfect, like a sonnet.
But where is Cesare? I need a shot
In which the Boss's hand is resting on it."
"Well, you, young lady," said Jerome, "appear
Possessed of just the thing your role demands.
Gracious! If only Cesare were here,
Or even just the part we need: his hands.
It seems it's AWOL Day here on the set.
Arkady's flown the coop, and where the hell
The Boss has gone is anybody's bet.
Still, don't you think we're doing pretty well?
Let's keep it up. We only get to borrow
These stylish premises until tomorrow."

117

It's dark, and Viña's vexed. "How many men
Have sung the praises of my silken thighs?
Yet will I never meet their like again,
Or ones who only go for hands and eyes?
It seems you wish to spare my fans the sight
Of all this droopy flesh and cellulite."
He laughs; she has incomparable curves.
"Time's passage, Viña, hasn't left a scratch
On you. But cellulite . . . now, that deserves
A closer look!" With this, he lights a match.
"Oh no!" she shrieks, "You'll set the bed afire!"
"As if we didn't do that every night,"
He says. "As if you weren't still my sole desire."
The match goes out. She rubs his belly. "Liar."

118

She had to go. Jerome just lay awake—
As in, "Awake forever in a sweet
Unrest"—not bittersweet, but wholly sweet,
His heart too full of gratitude to break.
By morning he's decided: *I must make*
Amends for all this marital deceit;
And though it's out of character, perform a feat
Of daring done for someone else's sake.
One hopes the gods of unrequited love
Are glad this old phenomenon survives,
And may incline toward helping Tom Jerome;
Perhaps arrange a not-so-gentle shove
To his behind. But look! When he arrives
At *Ristorante Viña*, no one's home.

119

No cast, no crew, no cameras in sight,
No sound equipment. *Gosh, I'll bet it's safe to say*
That something must have hit the fan last night.
I wonder what's the deal? Where's Cesare?
The bar is dark; atop the marble stair,
Jerome emits a laugh; no gloom and doom
For him. He asks aloud, "Is anybody there?"
And then the door swings open to the dining room;
An aged man moves toward a table by the wall—
His usual table, it would seem. It strikes Jerome:
The old man's footsteps make no sound at all.
He's wearing carpet slippers; this is *home*.
"The time has come, my friend, for you and me
To have a little chat," he says. "Do you take tea?"

120

"Please tell me if you would prefer *caffè*.
My man can bring you some. Good, here he is!
Aha! I see you've met the Russian, eh?
You've got to love that winsome smile of his.
Arkady, bring us tea, then say goodbye
For now." Jerome said, "I have seen you too,
Here, more than once," and nodded, "*Piacere*. I
Must confess, it seems I've lost my cast and crew.
As I recall, we're filming here today.
When I arrived just now, I was expecting
To find them hard at work with Cesare
Fumento. He's producing; I'm directing."
"Blame me," the old man said, "I sent them home.
You see, last night I spoke with Tom Jerome."

121

"Well, if you did," Jerome replied, "it must
Have slipped my mind. It could be true, and yet
It's hard for me to think that I'd forget.
You'll pardon me this little blip, I trust;
It comes with age, the mind accumulating rust."
The old man shrugged. "But you'd have won your bet
If you had wagered that we hadn't met.
That said, your larger bet is going bust.
Allora. Shall I fortify your tea?"
"A little early," said Jerome, "for me."
"You never know which drink will be your last,"
The old man said. "You should start drinking fast."
Jerome was thinking, *I can't help but feel*
We're nearing what is called "the Big Reveal."

122

"The Tom Jerome with whom I spoke last night
Is on the run from creditors; the law
Pursues him. I can see the time just might
Be ripe to borrow his identity. The flaw
Was not your plan. The flaw was you're an amateur
Who'll let his girlfriend's wishes wreck his chances.
A willingness to tell her 'no' is de rigueur,
As crime's more apt to kill you than romance is."
Jerome said, "Maybe you could fill me in
On my misdeeds before this goes too far."
"The list is long," the old man said, "But let's begin
With this: You aren't who you say you are."
Jerome replied, "This begs the question, if it's true,
Of who am I, but while we're at it, who are you?"

123

"I'm Viña's father and I own this place.
Two days ago, Arkady came to me
With quite the tangled tale, a standard case
Of someone harboring an enmity
Against a man who's treated him like dirt.
I don't mean you—he thinks the world of you!
It was my son-in-law he meant to hurt,
And so he told me everything he knew."
(Were this a movie, Marco might have done
A "two shot" here—we'd see these worldly men,
Their level gaze, each sizing up the other one.)
Jerome said, "Tell me, what's your name again?
I'd guess that what Arkady spoke was true,
But incomplete, so I'll be straight with you."

124

"So you'll be straight with me. I'm reassured.
I'm Amadeo Gallo. If you would,
Do tell me how my son-in-law procured
Your services, and why he ever would?"
"Alfeo introduced us, more or less.
We met right here and did some wining, dining.
He'd made some films, he said, with some success,
But lately found pornography confining.
So would I lend my talents to his dream
Of fashioning a work of art? Of course I would!
(Though not for art's sake—for the income stream.)
I'd steal his wife and flee the neighborhood
Before I'd ever have to fake the part
Of film director. Then, alas, my heart . . .

125

. . . got (shall we say) entangled in her hair,
Her breath, her lips, and if she said, 'I want
The moon, or just to be in movies,' there
You'd find me, filming in your restaurant,
Pretending, after all, that I was skilled
In cinematic arts. Your Viña'd be
An actress, even if it got me killed,
Or meant she'd never run away with me."
What's this?—Don Gallo smiled! "Don't cut your wrists,
Or rend your shirt, or even sing the blues.
A man who, at my daughter's asking, twists
Himself in crazy knots—that isn't news.
I've rarely known a fellow who resists
For very long when Viña turns the screws."

126

This information percolated, more
Or less, until at last the old man spoke
His mind. "I wonder what a woman's for
Sometimes. A joke is not a funny joke
When played on you a time or two or ten,
As with our Viña's wiles, which skew our lives
From what we'd planned again and yet again."
"You're talking to a man who's had four wives,"
Jerome replied, "and each one in her time
Enchanted me. They pale before her. I am
In Viña's thrall. But fatherhood!—a rocky climb
I'll bet it's been with Helen when you're Priam."
"I think," said Gallo, "Helen's dad was Zeus;
But sire a pretty daughter and all hell breaks loose."

127

"How odd that I recall a video
I made of her some twenty years ago.
A schoolgirl then, our Viña—was she fourteen?
Neither child nor woman—something in between
She was. If any hapless local boy,
Emboldened by his hormones, claimed to love
Her, I'd dispatch some younger iteration of
The useful types I currently employ
To shoo him off. But she was eager for the taste
Of things forbidden—eager just to leave.
The fingers of the world curled round her waist
And drew her, like the serpent leading Eve."
"If Viña had been Eve," Jerome replied,
"That serpent would have loved her till he died."

128

"All in all, you strike me as a cut above
The common run of Viña's suitors. Many
In number have they been, but few in love,
Which is to say there have been scarcely any
With whom I would have had a cup of tea
Before deciding what to do about
Some half-assed plan they'd hatched to steal from me.
It's good no harm was done, but when you flout
The rules we have against receiving wads
Of cash my son-in-law would blithely skim
Off my receipts, you're challenging the odds."
"But my intention was to steal from him,
Not you," Jerome replied, "What's more, I've earned my fee.
Just let me get this picture done. You'll see."

129

Don Gallo scratched his chin. "I am impressed
That you would ask permission to extend
An act of fraud to which you'd just confessed—
As if this escapade of yours need never end!
But now it's time for consequences, sad to say.
I get the feeling that for you this place
Is hardly real. It's real enough to Cesare.
So real, alas, he's terrified to show his face."
"*Signore,*" said Jerome, "What would it cost
To give your son-in-law a second chance?
This movie could revive a love he lost;
That's some extenuating circumstance!
Love's call is never easy to ignore.
It's not just something real; it's *something more.*"

130

"Allow me," said the Don, "to fill your cup.
I haven't asked your real name. Wonder why?
Because you'd simply make another up.
I know you're an imaginative guy.
Which makes me wonder, have you not been told
How Viña got involved with one so crude
As Cesare? He was a punk who trolled
For runaways and filmed them in the nude."
Jerome said, "Ah. Young love. You had to let him live.
If not, you would have risked a bigger loss."
"All true. What did I do? Demand they wed, and give
The SOB his chance to play 'the Boss.'"
Poor Gallo, thought Jerome, although the worst
Of it was finding out this film was not her first.

131

"At fifteen, Viña got an older gent
To help her run away, and off they went.
A doctor and a sober Lutheran—a Swiss!—
He threw it all away for just a kiss.
I felt for him. He caught no grief from me.
By fifteen she was Venus, rising from the sea.
In Rome she cut him loose, discarding said
Physician like a hat tossed on a bed.
He watched as she became a gangster's moll,
And in the end, OD'd on phenobarbital.
That day you met her, we had come to bury
This forlorn old doctor in the cemetery.
Love's call, you call it; it's a siren's song.
But come, you must have known this all along . . .

132

. . . and yet you're more than ready to succumb
Again each time you hear it, just the same.
I'd recommend a simple rule of thumb:
Choose not to listen. It's a sucker's game."
"But I've been thinking," said Jerome, "Ulysses
Took precautions, just as you might do.
With all respect, though, only sissies
Care that much about an extra day or two
Of ordinary life. To watch the clock's
Advance—that's not for me. I'd rather throw
Myself upon the mercy of the rocks,
And risk my all for rapture, even though
Innumerable men have run the risk before
And left their bodies on the sirens' shore."

133

"All right, then. No more Greek mythology.
And anyway, I'm just a businessperson
Who, as it happens, doesn't want to see
His daughter's marriage, or his cash flow, worsen."
But now the kid walks in. Jerome can tell
He thinks he's been betrayed. Yet to his own surprise,
Jerome is not afraid—just blue. He knows full well
He's much diminished in Alfeo's eyes.
Don Gallo says, "This kid has yet to learn
What makes the world go round. They're dopes,
These two—they're Rosencrantz and Guildenstern.
For this one, though, I'd had some higher hopes."
"He's young," Jerome said, "He got taken in.
Blame me, Don Gallo. Mine was the original sin."

134

"Sit down, kid," Gallo said. "There's no one here
To worry over. Think you're in a jam?
Relax. Feel free to speak, and have no fear
That you'll reveal my role; I've told him who I am."
"That so?" Alfeo said, "But who is *he*? We've not
Been introduced." Jerome thought, *This is where
The Don decides.* "Just call him Tom Jerome. Got
It? He's the master of the castle in the air,
But now—by which I mean three days from now, at most—
We'll see that film he's making. Cesare will host.
You, 'Tom Jerome,' will finish what you've started;
I'll not endure my daughter brokenhearted.
What was it Don Corleone said—'use all your powers'?
You'd better. You have seventy-two hours."

135

So, class dismissed. Outside now, on the street,
Alfeo says, "Your pompadour's a mess.
The old man really made you sweat. Confess."
"The Don? He made me hungry. Let's go eat."
The kid just laughs. "I know a place. We'll stop
And grab a nice *panino*. You can decompress—
Perhaps a glass of *grappa* too—unless
You'd rather order takeaway, and hop
A train to Zurich. Blowing out of town's
The strategy of choice for beating stress
When someone's in a bind like you. The ups and downs
Involved in duplicating past success
Are like a roller coaster when you try
To duplicate what was, in fact, a lie."

136

"You make it sound so calculating, kid,
When 'calculate' does not apply to half
Of what I said, and even less to what I did.
My lies are more like prayers—don't laugh!
They're just improvisations, my best shot
At wriggling through the moment, as I had
To do when you and Guildenstern once got
Me cornered in an Aventine hotel. Not bad,
Eh?—how I sensed you were a man who yearned
To be a star? And then you introduced
Me to my girlfriend's husband. I could see
That, with a plan, this could be big for me.
But Viña yearned for stardom too. That overturned
The plan, and now the chickens have come home to roost . . .

137

. . . including you, of course, but we are friends
Who understand the means can justify the ends.
And poor Arkady, sorely disrespected
Till he—like some Russian spy—defected.
And Cesare, the boss whom he betrayed,
In hiding now because of him, afraid
His glitterati world has gone to hell,
As have his chances for long life as well.
Of course, the Boss is not the only one
For whom the prudent thing might be to run.
But neither of us will—no, neither he nor I.
The means *can* justify the ends. I'll tell you why:
To cut the thread with Viña isn't worth
A few more ordinary days on earth."

138

"Jerome, I guess if anybody could defy
All hope and reason, you would be the guy.
I'd also guess you know what it will take
To make Don Gallo's heart go pitter-pat;
He has a soft spot for his daughter. Make
A little magic for her. Can you manage that?"
"I think I can, Alfeo. I won't lie
And say I'm confident, but you can help me try."
"That so? Remember when I had a cord
Removed from round your neck? Did you forget?
So now some further risk is my reward!
You're thinking, *Rosencrantz will go for that, I'll bet.*"
"I know you will," came Tom Jerome's reply.
"You want this movie made as much as I."

139

Jerome had gotten paid some weeks before
By Pio—dapper coffee bar habitué
And bagman for the big man, Cesare.
Here's Pio now. He's standing in the door
And peering through the crowded osteria
For those familiar Ray-Bans and that pompadour.
"Ah! Tom Jerome, *presumo*? Glad to see ya!
You're just the fellow I've been looking for!"
"And I'm invisible?" Alfeo said.
"Oh, no, it's just that you're already dead,
But don't yet know it, as the saying goes."
Jerome said, "Here for me, though, I suppose?"
The dapper one replied, "Yes, I was sent
To learn where you and all the Boss's money went."

140

"I hope a refund's not what Cesare—
A man who said his mind's on art—intends
To ask of me. Perhaps my résumé
Was padded just a trifle, but I'll make amends.
That bar where you and all your colleagues go—
Let's meet outside the place, tonight at ten.
I need to get my ducks all in a row;
Just ask the Boss to hold his fire till then."
"I'll see what can be done," said Pio; then away
He went. Jerome said, when they were alone again,
"My name is _____. Now you know.
But listen, we don't have a lot of time today,
And I've got something else needs doing. Go
Find Marco. Have him bring two cameramen . . .

141

. . . to Campo de' Fiori. You can tell
Him we'll be filming in the street tonight
The way we did before—we're going Nouvelle
Vague again—and once again in black and white.
And by the way, I'm Tom Jerome so far
As anybody knows among the crew.
If I'm deceived in that regard, it's au revoir
For me, and likely much the same for you."
"Come on," Alfeo said, "You think they'd mind
That much? Of course your name is counterfeit;
But what you bring is real. And if they find
You aren't Tom Jerome, you think they'd quit?
Look, no one cares about your little lie;
They care about the film. And so, by now, do I."

142

Who knew, Jerome was thinking, *that the son*
I never had would be a kid who earned his pay
In porno films? "You'd think it would be fun,"
Alfeo said. "It's more like Groundhog Day—
The grind," he sighed, "the grind. When Cesare
Needs muscle brought to bear on someone,
Me, I volunteer. A welcome getaway.
But then it's always back to business when I'm done."
They'd come to Circo Massimo. "This hill
Must rouse some memories," Jerome replied.
"Up there—the Aventine—is where we met,
And where I thought for certain you would kill
Me on the spot. Resourcefully, I lied."
"Hey, don't remind me. It could happen yet."

PART VIII

143

This town was built on seven hills. Of these,
The one he favored was the Aventine,
Where in the Garden of the Orange Trees,
As summer ended, something unforeseen
Occurred in this, *The Life of Tom Jerome*—
"A kiss," he now reminded her. "The ground
Just vanished under me, and I was 'on the foam
Of perilous seas.' How gladly I'd have drowned
Just then. You know it's never been a strength
Of mine, resisting when the siren sings,
But then the truth conforms to fit the length
And breadth of my imaginings."
"*Allora*," Viña laughed, "I'll pardon you in full
If just for once you'll spare me all the bull."

144

Fact is, she used a venerable Italian word
For "bull," then grandly flicked her cigarette.
Italian must be seen as well as heard;
He saw he wasn't off the hook just yet.
"You know, I nearly told you the essentials
That very night," he said, "that I am not
Above inflating my credentials.
But then we kissed, and truth just lost a lot
Of its appeal. I worried how you might respond
If I were just some ordinary guy
Who couldn't make a movie with a magic wand.
So I kept quiet. After that, I didn't lie—
I lied to others, yes, but not to you.
To lie when you're in love—that wouldn't do."

145

"That boy, the one whose grave you came to see—
The English poet—when his life was done,"
She asked, "how old was he?" Jerome replied,
"Just twenty-five. He died in eighteen twenty-one.
Consumption did him in. But for a century
Or two, his devotees have stood beside
His quiet grave in love and grief, and cried.
Their tears compose his immortality."
"Such talk!" she said, "I wonder why you dwell,
With all this extra time, on all this gloomy stuff.
You've had the years the boy did not. That's not a sin,
But Dante might have found a place in hell
For those who get the time, yet never go all in.
I'd hoped, for once, to get you off your duff."

146

"I should have never—" "Shhh," she said, "I do
Not hear confession—least of all from you.
What's more, I'd be impious if I said
You were absolved of sin, while we're in bed."
He laughed. She said, "We're both to blame,
Dismissing time as if we're in a game
Without an end." "It's true," he said, "The time I got,
I wasted, trying to be something that I'm not."
"You never tried to be; you claimed to be—
Until, that is, you got involved with me.
To see you go all in is what I'm all about.
It may be true you can't make something out
Of nothing, but you can make *something more*—
It's what the gods created muses for."

147

"You knew?" "Of course," she said, "I smell a rat
When someone tells me they're a film director.
You know how many men have told me that?
By now I am a walking lie detector.
My husband, though, he's easy to persuade
If you can get his male vanity involved.
It's what explains the big advance he paid
You; you're a mystery he has never solved.
But me—mere woman though I am—I've got
You figured out: a man who's genuine,
Accustomed to pretending that he's not.
This is the fix your indolence has got you in.
So thank me for the chance I've given you
To finally do what you were meant to do."

148

"I did try, Viña, back in Hollywood.
I'd hoped to get it right, but never could,
And wound up just another hanger-on
Who scarcely leaves a ripple when he's gone.
But here in Roma, under false pretenses,
I've tasted love and made a stab at art,
And bid that indolence of mine depart.
(Though now, of course, come consequences.)
But when you mention what I'm meant to do,
There's more than one thing, Viña; there are two.
To see you on the screen, to know I've done
You justice, as I promised: number one.
And two? You'll know it when I've pulled it off.
I'm sure, were I to tell you now, you'd scoff."

149

"Whatever it may be," she said, "I hope
It gets you off the hook with Cesare
And my *papà*, and with that hapless dope,
Alfeo." "Don't," he said, "forget Arkady.
Just making sure you cover everybody."
"Haha," she said, "You're like a bar of soap,
So slippery. I worry there will come a day . . . "
"And when it does," he told her, "You will cope."
She laughed, "How mean you are!" But they made love
In solemn fashion, knowing what he said was true—
That, come what may, she'd find a way to rise above
It. Still, the second thing he meant to do
Was leave her better off than she had been—
As *he* was, having gone, for once, all in.

150

Jerome found Marco. It was nearly ten.
"Surprise the bastard. That's what my advice is,"
Marco said. He'd brought along two cameramen
Equipped with handheld digital devices.
The darkling street near Campo de' Fiori:
A table, two chairs, vapor street lamps overhead.
Then out he came—the Boss, in all his glory.
"Don't shoot until I tell you," Marco said.
Jerome was waiting. Cesare assumed his chair.
The waiter brought two coffees, strong and black.
Alfeo stood behind Jerome; in this affair,
The dapper Pio had the Boss's back.
Some luck, Jerome was thinking, would be nice;
I'd really hate to have to do this twice.

151

The Big Man said, "You've got about a minute
To reimburse me every euro that I paid
You to direct a film with Viña in it."
Jerome said, "Come, you failed to make the grade
As our producer. Whichever way you spin it,
Your people turned against you. You're afraid
If it's a contest for their hearts, I'll win it,
And then you'll never get your movie made."
The Big Man, rising, said, "The money. Now."
"You mean Don Gallo's money? Just what's up
With you, to steal from him!? You're in a world of hurt,"
Jerome declared. "It looks like curtains for the cow
Of cash." With that, he calmly poured his cup
Of black espresso down the Big Man's shirt.

152

Imaginary monsters in the night
Aren't half so scary as that howling man
Who charged Jerome. His innards told him "fight
Or flight," though neither really fit his plan
Of hanging on until the camera guys
Could get their shot. But here his very life
Was pending under someone twice his size
Who yelled, "You fuck my wife? You fuck my wife?"
Oh, that'll do, Jerome decided—"Hands and eyes!"
He shouted, "Hands and eyes!" And in they darted,
Cameras rolling, Big Man raging, roaring, "Lies!
Bastardo! Ever since the day we started!"
Above the tumult, Marco bellowed, "Cut!
We've got it!" Cesare spun round—"Got what?"

153

But Tom Jerome commanded, "Keep 'em rolling,
Marco! Allow me to apologize
To Cesare. I took no joy, my friend, in trolling
You. We needed shots of hands and eyes,
And furious ones at that. You truly looked
Like an avenging angel, more enraged
Than even I could wish. *My goose is cooked*,
I thought! How perfect, though—your pain uncaged
Like that, a thing we'd never seen. The taunts—
The fight, the cameras—all a plan to get the Don
La cosa che vuole—the thing he wants,
Which ain't his money, but an image on
The screen that shows his daughter in the proper light.
For, after all, that's why we're here tonight."

154

"And out of what," the Boss inquired, "will you make
This film? The shoot at Campo de' Fiori,
Some footage from *il ristorante*? It'll take
A whole lot more than that to tell your story.
A feature runs how long—two hours? That
Just isn't in the cards, unless you know
Some way to pull a rabbit from a hat."
"The rabbit is a music video,"
Jerome replied. To which the Boss, unable—
So it seemed—to go ballistic anymore,
Just sighed: "I order dinner and I get dessert.
Alas." But then he reached across the table,
Snatched away that celebrated pompadour,
And calmly mopped the coffee from his shirt.

PART IX

155

"As gestures go," Jerome said later, "that
Was something, though I wish I'd worn a hat."
Alfeo said, "Let's hope that you can find
Another hairpiece, or we'll all go blind!
The glare—*marone!*" And everybody howled
With laughter at the way the Boss had toweled
His shirt with this poor bastard's bad toupee.
"It's time, though," said Jerome, "for me to say
A thing or two I should already have confessed."
But Marco said, "You think we hadn't guessed?"
And everybody laughed again, and jeered
Superbly; it was nothing like he'd feared.
"I'm glad you guys have actual skills," he said.
"I only have this vision in my head . . .

156

. . . which I have lacked the confidence to share
Till I was certain we could get away
With it. But now we know that Cesare
Will settle for a handful of my hair.
Let's give him something more than that—don't laugh!—
A tale of lust and loathing, fear and woe,
And love's redemption—in a video
That runs, at most, four minutes and a half.
A full-length feature film could not depict
So much so economically, whereas
Our video will be a sudden storm, which has,
Like love, an ending that you can't predict.
A swanky restaurant is where it's set,
With glamorous clientele on hand, and yet . . .

157

. . . our heroine, the owner's wife, could use—
She thinks—a thrill or two. So what's the score?
We've seen the dailies, so I've got some news
For her: The storm's about to come ashore.
So far, the evening's going uneventfully;
As usual, she sets the room aglow. But here's
Her husband, watching her resentfully,
Though truth to tell, they haven't shared a bed in years.
Now, in walks sexy here, and off we go.
Just look at her; we've caught her unawares.
You've got the footage—Viña down below
Among the tables, and the kid atop the stairs.
He strikes his gangster-in-tuxedo pose
And BOOM! She's all at sea. That's all she knows."

158

"The storm is in her mind," said Marco. "There-
fore, in her mind is where we'll set the scene.
We're flying digital, by which I mean
This crew will give you fairy dust to spare;
You've only got to fling some in the air
And we'll compose, from pixels on a screen,
As stormy an affair as ever there has been.
And it begins as he descends the stair . . . "
The kid is gorgeous, thought Jerome, *but who could miss*
The signs: that, more than movie stardom, what
He wants is just to be a part of this;
For in the end, the kid is still a kid.
It's plain to see the camera loves him, but
Unlikely any human ever did.

159

So: Marco and the editor, Antonio,
And others on the postproduction crew
At work past midnight on the video.
Jerome was thinking to himself, *They do*
Things I could never; work the stone, the clay—
But me, I'll be the someone to believe
In them and what they do, and come what may,
I'll have my moment too. A tug came on his sleeve:
"*Ma, scusi,*" Rafi said, "I do the sound.
And customarily, I would be told which song
We plan to build this video around.
That's reasonable, no? Perhaps I'm wrong."
"You're right. And more than one," Jerome replied,
"I've given this some thought. Let's take a ride."

160

The Big Man's club: still Dantesque despite
The fact that Cesare himself is on
Indefinite sabbatical tonight.
(Might there be issues pending with the Don?)
But Tom Jerome's not here to see the Big
Man—rather, someone lower down the chain.
"Can that be you?" she cries. "But where's the wig?
The man we're used to wears a lion's mane!"
They did that thing with kisses in the air;
He told her, "Amber, I am back again.
But you should know it's not your derriere
I'm here for—it's your cultural acumen."
She said, "You mean you have no use for me?"
He said, "The opposite is true. You'll see."

161

"When, on occasion, you've been in the throes
Of passionate romance," he said, "the men
Seemed steadfast at the start. A woman knows
What's coming, though—just not precisely when."
They shared a knowing look. He asked her then,
"Is there a song—perhaps an artist—who
You play when love's gone up in flames again?
I'm sure some feelings are particular to you.
There's heartbreak in this thing, and we could use
A song or two that speaks to that—the swell
And fall of love, the dreary repetition. Choose
The music we should play; on your behalf we'll tell
The way it feels to wish upon a star
When you are you and men are who they are."

162

"There *is* a man who sings his songs for me.
But more," she said, "I really shouldn't say.
One part of me, at least, belongs to me.
I hesitate to give that part away."
The sound guy, Rafi, said, "This man's a great
Director, here because he wants to spin
A truthful tale of love and women's fate.
And yet you hesitate." Jerome chimed in:
"I'm nothing of the sort. I'm just a guy
Who's learning late that it's a complicated
Business, all of this; I scarcely qualify
To speak for women. Your accumulated
Wins and losses, Amber, cannot be conveyed
Unless you give away a little. Still afraid?"

163

Outside he said, "That didn't take too long."
"It didn't?" Rafi laughed, "You closed the place."
"But look at what we got! We got the song,
We got the artist. Did you see her face?"
"I did, and all aglow for Jovanotti—
A pop star! Show me an Italian teen
Who wouldn't swear each song he ever wrote he
Wrote for her alone—completely sight unseen."
"But Rafi, that's the point. When Amber is alone,
Convinced that love and joy are what she'll never
Have for long, she makes this pop star's songs her own—
Her thing of beauty and her joy forever."
"*Ma certo*," Rafi said, "Why not? It must
Be what you mean when you say fairy dust."

164

"I've always liked him," Marco said. "His lyrics,
Sad to say, may be less than meet the eye,
But he's a wizard with love's atmospherics.
Alfeo, pull him up on Spotify."
The others moved in close; they'd spent a long
Night culling from the dailies bits and pieces,
Scraps of video that worked the best. A song,
And now another, played. *It never ceases
To amaze me, how by way of cogitations,
Serendipitous connections, lucky guesses,
Sudden patterns will emerge like constellations:
The thing that you were after coalesces.*
"But how did that just happen?" Marco said.
Jerome just smiled. "I'm going home to bed."

165

What'd he arrived at, working through the night?
What any sculptor dreams about: the shock
Of recognition when he catches sight
Of that which had been hidden in the rock.
He couldn't sleep. The story cut was done;
It had a rough-hewn beauty that, before
Too long, would speak its truth to everyone.
But not just yet; it needed *something more.*
"Ah!" Rafi cried, "You're back! The better to enrich
The runaway excitement that we movie elves
Are having, working on a video in which—
Oh, big surprise!—the actors play themselves."
"Not all of them," Alfeo said. "It seems
I'm playing you." Jerome just chuckled: "In your dreams."

166

"It's frame by frame now," Marco said, "We buff
And polish, sync the pictures with the sound,
Create a texture luminous enough,
They'll think the stars of old are still around.
The music's perfect; Jovanotti drives
The storm—to which we likened love—ashore,
With hip-hop rhythms as the storm arrives.
A storm it is, Tom—watch the monitor."
He did. *You're right*, he thought. *You're right.* And, silent
In the aftermath, the postproduction guys
And he all knew they'd pulled it off—the violent
Joy they wrestled with, the pride, the wild surmise.
Then Marco said, "This came while you were gone,
Apparently a package from the Don."

167

"You know what, Marco? It's our lucky day
If this is what I hope it is. And yet—
Have we got anything on which to play
A 20-year-old videocassette?"
The kid said, "That's a videocassette?"
And Marco laughed. Jerome did too. *I guess*
The measure of how old a man can get
Is if he still remembers VHS—
Or whether, like the Don, he's got a tape
He's kept and means to watch, but never does;
One made before his daughter's big escape
And capturing the butterfly she was.
He'd learned that he could never make her stay,
When butterflies are made to fly away.

168

"I wonder," said Alfeo, "why the Don
Would send a tape of Viña as a teen."
"Because he knows," Jerome replied, "upon
The spectrum of what can and can't be seen,
His daughter's inner light is infrared,
Which, as a rule, we lack the means to see.
He wants that light made visible, he's said,
And dreams this video of ours will be
A kind of lens. Instinctively, he knew it—
That when you look upon a work of art,
Your eyes are realigned; you see things through it,
So you are changed; and not just eyes, but heart.
Just think: How could that old paisan express
This better than by sending us that VHS?

169

Now Cesare appeared—a burly mound
Of laundry, sleepless since Arkady slipped
The knife in him a few days back. "No script!"
He said, "You had no script! I'd surely found
A reason I could end this thing—and right around
The time that Russian who betrayed me gripped
You by the throat. As usual you slipped
The noose. You must have thought that, pound for pound,
I was the dumbest man you'd ever met."
Jerome said, "I'm not sure the verdict's in just yet.
For if you've been a dummy, so have I.
We're men who want; we can't say what, or why."
So then, as melancholy as a fallen king,
The Boss said, "Now we are together in this thing."

170

"I've been dispatched—yes, this is what's become of me—
To ask you if your video is done.
If not, let's hope it's soon; the Don expects to see
Your masterpiece this afternoon, at one."
"*Our* masterpiece"—Jerome said—"Ours for sure."
"No, I'm a once-upon-a-time producer," said
The Boss, "and now an ex-restaurateur.
And by tonight, who knows?—I could be dead."
"A verdict!" Tom Jerome declared. "In all my life,
You are in fact the dumbest man I ever met.
And blind as well. For twenty years your wife
Has had your back, but you don't see it yet.
You really do believe the Don will kill you,
Or at the least, that your career is done . . .

171

. . . Restrain the urge to whine till later, will you?
At least until this afternoon, at one."
But Cesare just grumbled: "That's a laugh.
I had to call on Viña to negotiate
A truce with her *papà* on my behalf.
And now all I can do is sit and wait."
"And me?" Jerome replied. "I'm on my knees
In prayer! The only way this turns out well
Is if the Don is thrilled with what he sees.
If not, I'm—how to put this?—SOL.
But you, my friend, can rest at ease. Go tell
Don Gallo yes, we're done. We beat the bell."
The Boss laughed. "Here—since you've got time to spare,
Go find yourself another head of hair."

172

Who'd ever buy a hairpiece off the shelf?
Jerome had, once; he'd bought that pompadour,
And—all in all—had not done badly for himself.
But this occasion called for something more:
Bespoke, of course, except that one could scour
All of Rome and never find a craftsman who
Could fabricate perfection in an hour.
So something short of that would have to do.
And then his cell went off, and it was she.
Such complicated days, she said—"These men!"
And Tom Jerome forgot about his vanity
And wondered only could he see her—when?
"So much to say," she said, "unheard, unseen.
Come, meet me after in the Aventine."

A note on the songs that accompany
sonnets 176, 181 and 187 in Part X appears
on the last page of this book.

PART X

173

In *Ristorante Viña*, members of the cast
And crew—they must forget how chic this place
Has been; they have a job to do, and fast—
Are moving furniture to clear some space.
"I wonder," Marco's saying, "if that frescoed god
Pursuing virgins on the wall will get
Distracted, glancing at the floor—'That's odd,'
He'll say, 'there's someone setting up a TV set!'"
That someone is Alfeo, whose career
In pictures hinges on today's premiere;
Who's putting chairs in rows, who's pitching in,
More guileless and unguarded than he's ever been;
Who's singing Jovanotti songs aloud;
Who's, in a word—and for the first time—proud.

174

"You got the Boss's text?" a girlfriend says. "So be it:
No day off for us. He merely has to snap
His fingers; we come watch his video and clap."
"The nerve!" says Amber, but she cannot wait to see it.
Himself—though casually attired today—
He roams the premises in kingly mode,
That bearlike handshake his unspoken code
For "never bet against ol' Cesare."
But in steps Amadeo Gallo. Gloom
Descends. "Who said I wanted cast and crew
Attending? Have your people clear the room—
Except for you, and you, and you, and you."
That last "and you" is Viña, now on hand.
"Papà!" she gleams. "Your wish is our command."

175

Though ordinarily it makes no sense
To chase away a captive audience,
There was some logic in the thing he'd done:
He really was an audience of one,
For whether Tom Jerome would sink or swim
Was in the end, entirely up to him.
No need for folks to watch the video
And tell him what to think of it: He'd know.
His daughter smiled and said, "I understand,"
And when they took their seats, he took her hand.
But Cesare just stood and fumed. He shot
Jerome a glance that said, "Let's show him what we've got."
Alfeo pulled the drapes. *I'm not so sure I know*
Just what that is, thought Tom Jerome, *but here we go.*

176

And then the music starts, the bass guitar
Kicks in, the TV screen begins to glow.
He's looking tentatively at his star
And wishing she would just look back . . . but no.
This private screening—this *spettacolo*—
Is, at this moment, everything to her.
The men she's known—the archipelago
Of men—it is as if they never were.
She knows she's been revealed; the camera's crossed
Directly to her heart, and shown she's got
The femme fatale part down, but that it's cost
A lot. What's real in Viña's life? What's not?
She listens. Jovanotti's singing this:
It's time you pushed yourself out over the abyss.

[Song: *"Mi Fido Di Te,"* Jovanotti]

177

The camera's on the guests, who fail to see
Beneath the glamour. Really, all they want—
The video conveys this wordlessly—
Is cool cachet—a gangster's restaurant!
There's even some small possibility
That one night something violent might occur.
The owner's famous for his jealousy;
Could be he'll blow his stack right here, at her!
A lock of hair, as if the wind were rising,
Blows across her eyes. But she's indoors; it must
Be Marco's doing, cleverly devising,
As he'd promised, tricks to play with fairy dust.
More Jovanotti, singing: *What are you*
Prepared to risk? And now, as if on cue . . .

178

. . . we're seeing what the wind blew in: the kid!—for whom
A lie Jerome once told him in a hotel room,
To save his skin, turned out to be prophetic:
Onscreen, this kid's impossibly magnetic.
And as for Viña, brushing from her eyes
That wayward lock of hair, there's no disguise
For what has just walked in; this thing, despite
The pretty packaging, is love—her kryptonite.
But now here's more of Marco's magic, spun
From Tom Jerome's imagination: one by one,
Then faster, in a storm, the pixels blow away—
The glittering clientele, the glowering Cesare.
The real-life Viña, watching, sits and sighs
At what she sees—the lovers' hands and eyes.

179

She may be thinking this: My history
Is my advanced degree; the scars it's left behind,
They certify I've learned a thing or two or three
By now, and that I know my heart and mind.
But on the other hand, my heart and mind,
They make their own decisions, one, two, three—
And me, I'm doomed to tag along behind,
Not once, but every time. So much for history.
But look! Onscreen they circle close, and closer yet,
According to that slow, primordial etiquette
That rules the creatures of the seas and skies
(Not all of which have hands, but all have eyes).
And Viña, watching, leaning in to see
It's not her fault; it's only natural history.

180

Slow etiquette at first but, set to burst,
They touch—a scene rehearsed and re-rehearsed
Beginning (as the poet wrote it down)
" . . . in ancient days by emperor and clown."
Their fingers merely have to brush the skin
For us to know the crazy rush they're in.
The skin, the skin! The way her eyes grow wide,
The way her body goes all weak inside.
And though her history may tell her wait,
The flesh says *consummate, just consummate!*
A bath of dopamine: *I'm yours, you're mine,*
Is what the fingers say as they entwine.
So sweet, and yet we can predict what's coming:
The sight of those same fingers drumming . . .

181

. . . absently upon a tabletop, and eyes
Gone wandering in search of something fresh,
As men are always eager to hypothesize
The possibilities of other flesh.
For women, though, new love's another try
At "Joy, whose hand is ever at his lips
Bidding adieu; and aching Pleasure nigh,
Turning to poison while the bee-mouth sips."
Remember Amber? She's the one who told
Jerome how old this gets; it gets *so old*.
So here's a different song she thought would fit—
That doesn't let you think, that says to hell with it—
The lovers cursing in the street, their story
Going up in flames in Campo de' Fiori . . .

[Song: "*Il Sole Sorge Di Sera,*" Jovanotti]

182

. . . so that she tears herself away from him,
Is fleeing this way, toward us, through the mob.
Jerome remembers fearing for her life and limb,
But she'd said, "I'm an actress. It's my job."
He'd smiled, but he didn't tell her Cesare
Would play the husband who'd been tailing her.
He told himself it's in the cause of *vérité*,
But couldn't even guess what might occur.
For from the very start, there was a pair
Of Viñas and a pair of Cesares; they played
Themselves, so who could say exactly where
Or when some kind of history might be made?
The one pair watched the other in the video;
They had an inkling; still, they couldn't know.

183

The crowd's exuberant and boisterously cruel.
For men who're blowing off testosterone,
The woman in the azure dress is fuel;
She must be in the market—she's alone!
But Viña's having none of it. At bottom,
Men are dogs, they *all* come barking after you
And will behave whatever way will get 'em
Fed or laid. *I'm unafraid; it's nothing new.*
Right now, though, Viña's tugging off her shoes;
Try running over cobblestones in heels!
The men compete to see who's manliest.
She feels a hand—no, two hands—grabbing at her breast.
It's rather worse than she'd expected; she could use
A little help. The camera pans, reveals . . .

184

. . . her guy—the hands and eyes? the mating dance?—is
Nowhere to be found. Perhaps he got a case of nerves
Himself, or thought, "She'll have to take her chances.
She left *me*, so let her get what she deserves."
The crowd becomes a swarm. But she has not
Survived this long relying on men's self-restraint;
No, rather on the hard-won toughness that she's got.
She's not about to clutch her pearls and faint.
There's someone else who's watching with commanding
Presence, much like Giordano Bruno's statue standing
In the middle of the square. He's mulling, waiting—
Once a jealous husband, reevaluating:
They're every man she's ever met or seen,
How really different from them have I been?

185

What holds him back? Why wait to rush across
The square to come to Viña's aid? He must
Have thought you cannot be forgiving and be Boss.
Forget that now; he feels his heart combust.
And look! She sees him too! No rowdy soccer fan—
No loud and threatening mob of them—can scare
Her, but her husband, when he's angry, can.
She looks uncertain when she sees him there.
But now he's coming toward her, passing in
And out of shadow. Can she swear he isn't after
Her? But still she doesn't bend; she holds her chin
Up in the crush of bodies and the cruel laughter.
These men don't have a clue to what's in store—
Not till they see his hands and eyes and hear him roar.

186

It was, in fact, a cold dismissive frown
That he was wearing, so Marco used the shot
That, after Tom Jerome had poured espresso down
The Boss's shirt, the camera guys made sure they got.
A different time and circumstance, but true
To the event, and far more cinematic.
"It's Italy," Jerome had told the crew,
"We want his entrance bold and operatic."
The rest was simply what occurred that night,
As Cesare laid waste to all that throng
Of losers who had done his Viña wrong.
The people watching this in black and white
Are all but cheering in the dining room.
Jerome (still favoring his nom de plume) . . .

187

. . . thinks, *Not too shabby for a kid from Queens;*
Presenting Samson and the Philistines!
The loud heart-pounding music ends. Another,
Sweeter song begins. They rest against each other:
She, who's held her own tonight, and he, who
When decision time arrived at last, came through.
The camera circles round; we see her face.
And then a slow dissolve: another time and place,
But still it's Viña, all of fourteen, tousled, fair,
Those Renaissance eyes, that Florentine hair.
She's like a song that's waiting to be sung—
Her father's vision of his girl forever young.
Now, what to make of this *spettacolo?*
"That's her! That's her! That's all ye need to know."

[Song: *"A Te,"* Jovanotti]

188

The Jovanotti song is called *"A Te"*—
Which in Italian means "to you." *To you,*
To you, Jerome was thinking. No one spoke.
They listened, or perhaps they merely thought
About what they'd been part of or had made
Or merely seen; no, *all* had played a role
In what Papà had hoped to make: a lens
Through which to see his daughter as she was—
Her inner light—in infrared. The old man kissed
Her hand in courtly fashion; then he bowed
His head. Her husband cleared his throat,
A guy who in the past had had men killed,
And pornographic movies made, but had,
Of late, been humbled just a bit. He spoke.

189

"So many are the movies I have seen
In which a woman's skin was all that I perceived.
That's all there is, was all that I believed.
But I've been shown just now how blind I've been.
And likewise, though I sensed, I could not see
Through all my selfish, coked-up nights and days
I was denying what my heart was telling me:
I love you, Viña. Let me change my ways."
He turned, as if to strains of *La Bohème*,
And wept. Then so did Viña. Like a bride,
She fell into his arms and cried and cried.
These two are so Italian, both of them,
Jerome observed, a tad ambivalent.
I got it done, though, didn't I? And out he went.

PART XI

190

Take notes, he thought. *It's easy to forget
The way it really was. Attend, keep track—
So you'll remember when you're looking back.
This old hotel, the room, the bed. (I'll bet
If people knew about the night we met,
They'd hang a fine commemorative plaque.)
To be here in the moment is a knack
Worth having, for a moment's all you get.*
And in she walked. "My movie star," he said.
She came and tendered him a pair of kisses,
One past either cheek, the way you'd greet a guest.
They lingered near, but not upon, the bed.
"It seems that I'm officially a Mrs.
Once again. So starting now I'm on my best . . .

191

. . . behavior." "Well, there's still no need to stand,
Nor any further need," he said, "for explanations.
Who can say what's certain when it comes to lovers and
Their feelings and their feelings' permutations?"
Hah!—that one broke the ice. "I guess," she said,
"There isn't any law that says we can't
Just have a conversation on the bed.
Besides, a man of your age has but scant—"
"Regard for —" he began, but she said, "Quiet, you—
Abandoning the room without an *au revoir.*
We showed the video to all the cast and crew.
They stood and cheered for me—and you! 'Our movie star!'
And then—you never would have guessed—
My husband turned to me and said, 'I'm blessed.'"

192

So I suppose, where Cesare's concerned,
I am—Jerome was thinking—*finally off the hook.*
But does the Don as well believe I've earned
My pay? I'll have to take it crook by crook.
Then Viña said, "There's something I should share.
When everyone had gone, we had a cup
Of tea, Papà and I. He said, 'Are you aware
That for your happiness he gave you up?'
And I said, 'You're a canny one. You knew.
Tom isn't who he said he was, and yet
He had two worthy things he meant to do:
The first, to let me glow onscreen. I'll bet
The second was to win me. But in lieu
Of that, to leave me better off than when we met.'"

193

She lay back on the bed. Jerome did too.
He draped his arm across her waist. He thought,
Take notes. "You haven't told me—how'd I do?"
She turned her head, the Baccarat they'd bought
Her swirling through him like a siren song.
"You did just fine," she said, relying not
So much on words as hands and eyes. "Come along,"
They sang: "The moment's all we've got."
So yes, for old times' sake, what love they made,
While off the open casements ricocheted
That famous Roman sun, and in the palm
Tops chattered parakeets. She whispered, "Tom,
You are the only man with whom I've ever been
The muse I wish I were. We went all in."

194

The bellman said, "Oh, I remember you;
I'm sure that hoodlum over there does too."
Jerome caught sight of him; thought, *This is good.*
Don Gallo didn't send the Russian, knock on wood.
"Here, thanks for looking out for me," he told
The bellman. "Seems I'm getting kind of old
For escapades. I should be satisfied, in fact,
To have my limbs and loins and wits intact."
He crossed the courtyard. "*Buona sera*, kid. Got
Any news for me?" Alfeo said, "A lot."
"At least it's you delivering it. Arkady—
By now, he'd be disposing of my body."
The kid said, "Not to worry. I won't bore
You with details. Arkady? Won't see him no more."

195

"You don't say. Should I ask at whose suggestion
This was done?" The kid replied, "Not every question
Gets an answer. But you know about this kind of thing.
As someone said, 'When you come at the king,
You best not miss.'" Jerome thought, *Life and art*
Among these guys are really hard to tell apart!
"So what's the news?" he said. "Has Cesare
Been warned he's got a fortune to repay?"
Alfeo drew a long inhale and tossed
His cigarette. "The Don is picking up the cost.
But I've got bigger news, and this is it.
I want to be an actor, so I've quit."
"You have?" "Why? Don't you think that I was good?
But where to make it happen—here or Hollywood?"

196

Jerome said, "No more porn? And no more crime?
You really mean to go legit this time?"
"Don't laugh. It's you who showed me what I wanted.
So who's to blame if I'm consumed and haunted?"
"Haunted! Gracious! Listen, kid. You're not the first
To catch the bug, and as an actor, not the worst.
So get yourself a passport. Take a shot
At Tinseltown and find out what you've got.
I knocked around the industry for years.
I've seen the qualities on which careers
Are made; they're many and they're various.
Young actors' lives can be precarious,
But till you're out there you will never know
Your chances: Go.

197

Your calling card's the video;
If 'leading man' is new to you, it doesn't show.
You leap right off the screen, and smart execs
Will know exactly what you're selling: danger, sex,
A smile to die for and—they'll sense this too—
That deep down, women want to mother you.
They'll think James Dean, but Dean was always acting.
Your cool is born and bred; just *matter-of-facting*.
I'd make some calls to help you if I could,
Except I'm less than loved in Hollywood.
So here you go—to pay the rent and buy a meal.
It's half of what I got; a deal's a deal."
Alfeo, wide-eyed, took the envelope.
It looks like money. What it is, is hope.

~ 128 ~

198

"But listen, kid"—Jerome inquired—"I
Forgot to ask your co-star if this did the trick.
She got the urge for acting. Did we satisfy
Her? It can get to be a need, and quick."
"The Don's the one who knows," Alfeo said.
"He sent me here to tell you that he dug
The video—he called it *infrared.*
So there's another victim of the movie bug!
He says to stay. Don't underestimate Papà;
That old paisan has people everywhere
In Rome and at—it's safe to say—Cinecittà.
Star Viña in a film, he says, and make it there."
This had Jerome in stitches as they said farewell.
"What's that they say about the road to hell?"

PART XII

199

He knew you never get your every wish,
But Tom Jerome decided that a man
Of his accomplishments deserves a dish
Of hazelnut gelato. In a span
Of ninety days or so he'd gone from "might
Have been" to "this is what it's like to be."
He'd screwed up early but he'd made it right,
And even got the girl—if temporarily.
So back here in Testaccio, he bought a scoop
Of hazelnut, and thought about that group
Of scoundrel artists whom he'd got to know
And how, because of him, they'd made a video.
There will be proof of sorts that he was here,
And for the friends he'd made, a souvenir.

200

The meadow by the old Aurelian wall
Was where they buried, at the Pope's decree,
Those sorry travelers—non-Catholics, all—
Who while in Rome fell prey to their mortality.
Above, a marble pyramid had towered
For two thousand years. Children played,
The sheep would graze, the daisies flowered.
And here, some decades later, Keats was laid.
He died in Joseph Severn's arms, a friend
Whose guileless generosity belied
Heroic depths of feeling. With him till the end
He was, and now he's buried by his side.
Here on the wooden bench before their graves
Sits someone; when she spots Jerome, she waves.

201

Jerome in Ray-Bans, leather jacket, jeans—
Essentially the same ensemble as before.
"Still," Amber said, "I miss the pompadour."
"Oh, that was catnip to the girls in Queens,"
He said. "But this—another off-the-shelf
Toupee. It's mortifying to a great artiste."
But she said, "I don't mind it in the least.
I go for seedy older men myself."
He laughed. "I think you've found the sine qua non
Of seedy older men. You gave me something, though.
Now take this in return, so you can have a look
At Keats's verse when me and my toupee are gone.
You gave me Jovanotti's art; my video
Contained your secret heart. Mine's in this book."

202

She studied Keats's tombstone. "*Ma dov'è
Il suo nome?*"—Where's his name? He said, "Our boy
Believed his name was 'writ in water.' Here today,
Then gone for good, like Youth and Life and Love and Joy."
"How sad," said Amber. "Every day is fine.
I hate to close my eyes for fear I'll miss one."
"Keats was robbed of his. I'd give him one of mine
If that were possible—though not, I must say, this one."
"No, not this one. Let's keep this one," Amber said.
They took a stroll, the graveyard densely populated
By the chatty spirits of the happy dead
Who'll never need to leave their paradise behind.
And she said, "What's your real name?" Now he hesitated.
But then she told him hers. And changed his mind.

THE END

Appreciation

For their contributions, whether they knew it or not, the author
would like to thank Jon Anderson and the alumni of Bear Mountain
Writers; Susan Becker; Elsa Proverbio-Bradford; Frances, Alice,
Jacqueline, Beatrice, and Nellie Bray; Amy Brown and Nathan Gageby;
Ed Zahniser; Elizabeth Casman; George Clack; Hali Taylor; Sollace
Mitchell; Amanda Thursfield; Nicholas Stanley-Price; Curtis Copeland
and Cheryl Shanks; Lee Underwood; William Lanouette; Libby
Howard; Tom Conant; Elisabetta Lazarte; Anita Miller; Tony Bennett;
Randall Tremba; Wendy and Stan Mopsik; Francesca Malagutti, Oscar
Porcelli, and the townsfolk of San Benedetto Po; and Brenda Thorne
and Wayne Bronson. And of course, Mary Ellen O'Connor, Caroline
and Christopher Smith, Lizzie and Jake Larson, and Tory and Dan
Martin. In addition, the shades of Seymour Altman, Ruth Deborah
Rey, Clara Facey, Jack Hashian, Katherine (Sammy) Leach, Doris Betts,
J.R. Salamanca, Jerry Ackerman, Margaret M. Casey, Ashley Cohn,
Richard Harter Fogle, Faye Wray, Miss Cummings, Fanny Brawne, C.
Hugh Holman, Joseph W. Houppert, Frank Sinatra, Ava Gardner, Marty
Robbins, James Salter, Joseph Severn, Tim Buckley, Arnold Stanton,
Betty and Dan Townsend, and Mary Anne and Wayne Wallace. And
John Keats.

A Note on the Songs in Part X

These three songs by Jovanotti go along with a trio of sonnets in Part X. You can look up the songs on YouTube (using the title of each song plus the word "lyrics") or use your cell phone to read the QR codes, which will take you directly to them.

To "read" the QR code, simply open the camera app on your cell phone and focus on the QR code as if taking a photo.

Sonnet 176
"Mi Fido Di Te"

Sonnet 181
"Il Sole Sorge Di Sera"

Sonnet 187
"A Te"